CHIHUAHUA CONSPIRACY

Pet Whisperer P I

.

MOLLY FITZ

Sweet Promise Press
PO Box 72
Brighton, MI 48116

ABOUT THIS BOOK

My crazy old Nan loves making decisions on a whim. Last week, she took up flamenco dancing. This week, she's adopted a trouble-making Chihuahua named Paisley. This wouldn't be much of a problem were it not for the very crabby tabby who also lives with us.

Man, I never thought I'd miss hearing Octo-Cat's voice, but his silent protest is becoming too much to bear, especially since we just opened our new P.I. business together.

Things go from bad to worse, of course, when Nan and I discover that someone has been embezzling funds from the local animal shelter. If we can't find the culprit soon, the shelter may not be able to keep its lights on and those poor homeless pets won't have anywhere to go.

Okay, so I just need to find the thief, rescue the animals, and save the day—all while trying to find a way for Octo-Cat and Paisley to set aside their differences and work together as a team. Yeah, wish me luck…

AUTHOR'S NOTE

Hey, new reader friend!

Welcome to the crazy inner workings of my brain. I hope you'll find it a fun and exciting place to be.

If you love animals as much as I do, then I'm pretty sure you're going to enjoy the journey ahead.

Chihuahua Conspiracy is just one of my many brain-tickling adventures! Many more will be coming soon, so make sure you sign up for my newsletter or download my app to help you stay in the know. Doing so also unlocks adorable pictures of my own personal feline overlord, Schrödinger, deleted scenes from my books, bonus giveaways, and other cool things that are just for my inner circle of readers.

You can download my free app here:
mollymysteries.com/app

Or sign up for my newsletter here:
mollymysteries.com/subscribe

If you're ready to dive right in to more Pet Whisperer P.I., then you can even order the next books right now by clicking below:

Chihuahua Conspiracy
Raccoon Racketeer
Himalayan Hazard
Hoppy Holiday Homicide
Retriever Ransom
Lawless Litter
Legal Seagull

And make sure you've also read the books that come before *Chihuahua Conspiracy* in the series. They can be read in any order, but you'll enjoy yourself more if you start at the beginning!

Kitty Confidential
Terrier Transgressions
Hairless Harassment
Dog-Eared Delinquent
The Cat Caper

And don't miss these special collections!

Pet Whisperer P.I. Books 1-3
Six Merry Little Murders

Okay, ready to talk to some animals and solve some mysteries?

Let's do this!
Molly Fitz

To anyone who wishes she could talk to her animal best friend…
Well, what's stopping you?

CHAPTER ONE

Hi, I'm Angie Russo, and this last year has been quite the wild ride for me. Yes, it's been exactly one year since my entire life changed for the better.

Sure, I've come face-to-face with a lot of dangerous characters lately—murderers, kidnappers, creeps, you name it—but I wouldn't trade my life for anyone else's.

Here's the deal… It all started at my former job as a paralegal.

A wealthy old woman had just died, and her heirs had gathered at our office for the official will reading. I was instructed to make coffee, and, well, that was the last time I ever attempted such a dangerous feat.

You see, I got electrocuted and knocked unconscious. I woke up with a wicked fear of coffee makers—oh, and also the ability to talk to animals. At first, I could only talk to this one cat named Octavius Maxwell Ricardo Edmund Frederick Fulton. He was one of the primary beneficiaries of his late owner's estate, and I now call him Octo-Cat for short.

Long story short, he told me the old lady was murdered and begged me to help him catch the killer. We did, and we pretty much became best friends in the process. Now he lives with me, and I oversee his care and also his generous trust fund.

And because I accidentally made an open-ended deal with him when I needed to get him to wear a pet harness, we now reside in his former owner's exquisite manor house. Yes, a ten-dollar neon green harness ended up costing me a cool million.

At least most of the money was my cat's, anyway.

Yeah. A lot has happened over the last year. My cat and I solved three more murders together. He got catnapped. I finally quit my paralegal job so we could open up a private investigation firm together, and oh, yeah… I got a boyfriend!

My nan might be even more excited about that one than I am. She'd been trying to matchmake me for years, and now that she's finally succeeded, she's not quite sure what to do with herself.

Yes, she continues to bake up a storm in the kitchen and take her community art classes, but lately she's also been flipping through new hobbies like they're going out of style. There's been flamenco dancing, learning Korean as a second language, even Pokémon Go. She claims Pikachu understands her on a spiritual level. Personally, I don't get it.

My mom and dad are busy with their jobs as Blueberry Bay's local news anchor and designated sports guy. Nan and I have them over once per week for a nice home-cooked meal. Did I mention my grandmother and I live together?

It's not weird. She's not just the woman who raised me, but she's also my best friend and the most amazing person I know. She even helps with Octo-Cat's lavish demands and rigorous schedule.

And between the two of us, we keep him dining on only the seafood flavors of Fancy Feast and drinking Evian from his favorite Lenox teacup.

Most recently, he's demanded a brand-new iPad Pro. His reasoning? That he needed a professional upgrade to go along with our new business venture. Never mind that he uses his tablet primarily to play various fish tank and koi pond games.

He's given his old device to the president of his fan club, a raccoon who lives under our front porch. His name is Pringle, and he's a pretty all right guy most of the time. Octo-Cat definitely enjoys having a fanboy to support every single decision he makes, including his regular criticism of me.

It's true. Octo-Cat complains a lot, but I also know he loves me tons. That's why I'm planning a special evening to celebrate our petaversary. I'm not sure he remembers, but after tonight he will.

I can't wait to see the look on his little kitty face when he sees what I have planned for him. Let the games begin!

I t wasn't easy hiding my party preparations from Octo-Cat, but so far he hadn't managed to catch on. Rather than cooking something myself, I asked Nan to pick up some grilled shrimp and lobster rolls from the Little Dog Diner in Misty Harbor. It's a bit of a drive, but worth every mile.

Nan would be returning any minute, which meant it was time for me to wake the guest of honor. I found him sleeping in his five o'clock sunspot on the western side of the house. "Wakey, wakey!" I cried in a sing-song voice he loathed.

"Angela," he groaned, "haven't you ever heard that you should let sleeping cats lie?"

"I'm pretty sure the expression is—you know what? It doesn't matter. C'mon, I have a surprise for you."

Whoa, close one. I almost used the word dog in a sentence. That little slipup would have ruined our whole night, but I caught myself just in time.

"A surprise?" he asked, yawning so wide

that his whiskers overlapped in front of his nose. "What is it?"

"You'll see. C'mon." I patted my leg and motioned for him to follow.

But he sat his butt back down on the hardwood floor and flicked his tail. "Tell me, or I'm not coming," he demanded.

"Octo-Cat, can't you just—Ugh, fine. Today marks one year since we first met. Do you remember that day?"

"So you mean it's been one year and one day since Ethel died?" he asked, raising his eyebrows and staring me down.

Oh, I didn't think of that. I hoped he wouldn't be too sad to celebrate.

"I'm just giving you a hard time," he said with a cruel laugh, trotting over as he shook his head. "Happy anniversary, Angela. I'm glad you're my human."

Footsteps sounded on the porch. I hadn't even heard Nan pull up, but now she was here, and we could officially begin our little party. I'd asked my boyfriend, Charles, to wait a couple hours before he turned up, since he and Octo-Cat didn't get along particularly well as of late.

I secretly loved that my cat was jealous of my boyfriend but hoped that he'd eventually get over it.

"Nan?" I called when Octo-Cat and I reached the bottom of the stairs, but she still hadn't entered. Padding over to the door, I twisted the knob and—

A wagging ball of black fur pounced into the house.

"I'm here! I'm home! Oh, boy. Oh, boy. Oh, boy!" the little dog cried, then immediately squatted and peed on the welcome mat.

I turned to Octo-Cat, who stood on the last stair with his back arched and his tail at full-blown puffball status. "Angela, what is this?" he screamed, unwittingly drawing the dog's attention over to him.

"A cat! A cat! Oh, boy! Oh, boy! Oh, boy!" The dog, who upon closer examination appeared to be a Chihuahua, bounded right up to Octo-Cat and pressed his nose to the cat's butt.

Octo-Cat hissed, growled, swiped with his claws, and sent the little dog shrieking away.

Yipe! Yipe! Yipe!

"What's all this commotion?" Nan asked,

charging into the house, spotting the little black dog and scooping the poor, whimpering baby into her arms. "Okay, fess up. Who hurt my Paisley?"

"Nan…" I pinched the bridge of my nose to stave off the rapidly building headache. "Why is there a dog in our house?"

"This is Paisley. Yes, she is," Nan cooed in a baby voice, and the Chihuahua licked her cheek, the horrible, scary cat and the pain he'd inflicted apparently forgotten. "She lives here now."

"Oh, heck no!" Octo-Cat shouted from his spot on the stairs. "I thought we were celebrating me tonight, not taking a visit to the ninth circle of hell!"

"Nan," I said trying to make peace before everyone lost their cool. "We can't have a dog here. Octo-Cat hates dogs."

"Hatessssssss," Octo-Cat hissed, then growled again.

"He hates me?" the shivering little dog asked. "He doesn't even know me. I'm Paisley, and I'm a good girl."

Nan continued to talk in a goochie-goo voice, keeping her eyes glued to the mostly black tri-color Chihuahua in her arms. "Well, I saw this little girl at the shelter and right away she stole my heart. What was I supposed to do?"

She looked up and narrowed her eyes at me. "Was I supposed to let her stay in that cage all by herself? Or, Heaven forbid, let them put her down when the shelter got too full?" She covered Paisley's oversized ears and frowned at me.

"No, I mean..." I sputtered. "No, of course you couldn't do that." Ack, I was such a softie.

"Octavius is just going to have to get used to his new housemate, because I'm not taking her back," Nan said in a way that made it more than clear that this topic was not up for discussion. "C'mon, baby, let's go outside and meet the forest creatures."

Once Nan and Paisley were safely outside, I searched around for Octo-Cat so I could both explain and apologize on Nan's behalf.

But he was nowhere to be found.

Crud, he was never going to forgive me for this one.

CHAPTER TWO

I found Octo-Cat at last in my bedroom, where he was crouched under my bed, his wide amber eyes glowing in the darkness. When I flopped down on my belly to get a closer look, he emitted a low growl that made me jump in my skin.

"Go away," he added in a rumbly, somewhat terrifying voice.

"That's not fair," I enunciated as if scolding a petulant child. "Might I remind you that I was just as shocked by that as you were."

I searched my brain for the right way to spin things, the way that would make him understand. Unfortunately, all logic tended to go out the window whenever Octo-Cat was unhappy—and today's unhappiness had already reached a record-breaking level.

With great difficulty, I managed to put a happy-go-lucky smile on my face as I said, "But, I mean, if you think about it, it kind of makes sense. Right? We have each other, and now Nan has a best fur friend of her own, too. Isn't that nice?"

"No," the tabby replied stubbornly and turned his face toward the wall.

I hated that he was this upset, but there was nothing I could do without him being willing to at least meet me partway. "Will you at least come out for our petaversary?" I begged, practically whined.

Octo-Cat turned toward me again; his eyes still held that eerie glow as he considered my request. "I'm not coming out," he said at last. "But if you bring my shrimp and my Evian here and promise not to let that dog in, I shall consider sharing the celebratory meal with you in our private quarters. *Privately.*"

I couldn't help but sigh. "Are you really not going to leave the room at all?"

He flicked his tail, waking a cloud of dust and pet hair that rose from the carpet in a sickening flurry. Wow, I really was not a good housekeeper.

If Octo-Cat noticed the filth, he didn't seem to mind—not when he already had much bigger fish to fry. "Not until that inter-loper is gone," he informed me with another hiss. "Need I remind you that this is MY house?"

"No, you needn't." It felt strange using Octo-Cat's overly refined language, but he often listened better when I did. And right now, I needed him to understand that control-ling Nan was every bit as difficult as trying to control him. Both were so stubborn about the things they wanted that we would have no choice but to find some kind of compromise to the Chihuahua situation.

I sighed again. "However, given your stance, it would probably be best if I brought your litter box up here as well. I'll be back in a little bit."

After pushing myself back into a standing position, I left my tower bedroom, careful to latch the door fully behind me. As much as I didn't want to trap Octo-Cat inside, I was also incredibly worried about what might happen to Paisley if she nosed her way in there. She was half his size at most and clearly didn't have an aggressive bone in her whole body.

My cat on the other hand?

He had a whole skeleton's worth.

I found Nan in the kitchen setting out a pair of dog bone-printed ceramic bowls for Paisley in a spot just to the left of the pantry. "Sorry about Octo-Cat," I muttered, ignoring the fact that he would be upset that the dog's bowls were so near his stash of Fancy Feast.

"That cat was mean," the Chihuahua whined as she rubbed at the fresh claw wound on her nose.

"He didn't mean to hurt you. He's just difficult sometimes," I offered with what I hoped was a reassuring smile.

The little dog jumped up and pawed frantically at my leg, wiggling her whole body as she cried, "Hey! Hey! Hey! Did you just talk? Do you know how to talk? You're a very good, very smart girl!"

I bent down and scooped her up, and Paisley immediately set to licking my face as if it were covered in gravy or bacon grease or some other irresistible treat. "Yes, I can talk to both animals and people," I explained. "I don't know why, though. It's kind of just the way things are. Would it be okay if I talked to you?"

Paisley wagged her tail so hard her entire body shook, then she broke apart into a shivering fit. Whether she needed a sweater or some anti-anxiety medicine, I couldn't say for sure. The shivering continued as she jumped into an excited monologue. "I've always wanted my own humans, and now I even have one that talks! The other dogs back at the shelter won't believe it! When are they coming for a visit? Or, oh! Maybe they could move in with us, too. This house is plenty big, and there are lots of dogs that need homes."

I laughed at her enthusiasm, even though her reminder of all the homeless pets that had remained behind following Nan's impromptu adoption of Paisley made my heart feel heavy. "I'm sorry, Paisley. I wish I could adopt all your friends, but I already made a promise to take care of my cat the best I can, and he would be very upset if we filled our house up with dogs."

As soon as I set Paisley back on the floor, she curled up against my foot and pouted. "He's a very mean kitty."

"Yeah, he kind of is, but he'll grow on you, I promise. And I bet you'll grow on him, too. He just needs time to get used to having you here. It's a very big change."

"It's a big change for me, too." The little dog ran in a circle to indicate the giant manor in which she now lived. "At the shelter I had to share a cage with two other dogs. It was very crowded. That's why I thought we could give some of the others a home, too."

Three to a cage?

I hadn't spent much time at the local animal shelter, but from what I remembered, we'd never had an overcrowding problem in the past. Maybe things had just been a bit different for Paisley than the others due to her extremely small size.

I already felt guilty about not being able to adopt more animals. Thinking of them now all cramped together made me feel that much worse. Maybe a few volunteer shifts or a small donation were in order, both to help them out of a potentially tough spot and to ease my guilty conscience.

"Hey," I said, crouching down so that Paisley and I were at closer to the same level. "How would you like to visit the shelter with me tomorrow? You can say hi to your friends, and I'll see if there's anything we can do to help them find new homes."

Paisley let out a high-pitched cry and began to shake furiously once again. "You're not making me go back. Are you?" the dog yelped. "Because Nan said this is my home now."

This poor thing. No wonder Nan had been charmed enough to bring her home.

"Oh, sweetie. I promise I wouldn't do that to you. Nan's right. This is your home now, and nothing's going to change that."

Paisley stood on her hind legs and reached her paws up my leg. "I love you, new mommy," she said. "This is the best day of my entire life."

My heart swelled at the Chihuahua's confession of love. It had taken me almost dying at the hands of a gun-toting psychopath to get Octo-Cat to even admit he liked me. Yet Paisley had only needed a single short conversation to forge the deepest of bonds. As much as I adored my Octo-Cat, it sure felt nice to be appreciated rather than insulted.

Hmmm. Maybe I'm not as much of a cat person as I once thought.

Of course, I immediately felt guilty for thinking that even in passing. It was our petaversary, after all, and I'd promised my feline overlord freshly grilled shrimp by way of celebration.

It was time to leave Nan and Paisley to celebrate their own adoption day together while I did my best to ease the poor, put-out kitty that sat waiting for me in my bedroom tower.

I closed my eyes tight and wished that one day we could all be one big happy family. I didn't have a candle to blow out and it wasn't anyone's birthday, but I hoped the special wish magic I'd grown up believing in could save us now.

Honestly, we were going to need a miracle to get my stubborn cat to change his heart when it came to the poor, shivering dog that needed us.

Just in case, I said a quick prayer, too.

One way or another, we would find a way to all live peacefully together.

After all, we didn't have any other option.

CHAPTER THREE

When I returned to my room with grilled shrimp and Evian for both Octo-Cat and myself, I found him sitting on my pillow flicking his tail pensively.

The moment he saw me, he popped to his feet and began to pace the length of the mattress. "Well, did you talk some sense into Nan about the unappreciated monstrosity she has wrought on our house? On my house?" He didn't even look at me as he spat each word. If he had, I'm sure my face would have given away everything he needed to know.

"Umm, a little," I hedged, trying hard not to sigh yet again. "Mostly I talked to Paisley, though, and she is really happy to be here."

Octo-Cat stopped pacing and stared at me with open disdain. "And I'd be really happy for her to *not* be here."

I let out a groan and sunk down onto the bed beside him. "I know change is hard, but—"

The tabby diva lifted a paw and shook his head. "I'll stop you right there. If you're not for me, then you're against me. And thus…" He paused and sighed heavily. "I bid you good night, Angela."

I watched helplessly as he hopped off the bed and crawled back beneath it. "Hey, I didn't ask for any of this, either," I called after him.

But Octo-Cat refused to respond.

"We can't just send her back. From what Paisley told me, the shelter is already pretty overcrowded, and that's not a very nice way for her to have to live, especially when there's a family who wants her. *Our* family."

He still said nothing to acknowledge me or my arguments.

"You can't just ignore me," I huffed, throwing myself back onto the bed in resignation. "How are we supposed to solve our cases if we're not talking to each other?" I asked while studying a smudge on the ceiling.

Octo-Cat didn't answer, which was probably for the best regarding this last point. The truth was even though we'd opened Pet Whisperer P.I. for business more than one week ago, we still had yet to book our first case.

If I could do it all over again, I might have rejected the kooky name that Mom and Nan had saddled us with. Around Blueberry Bay, calling yourself a pet whisperer pretty much guaranteed that folks thought you were crazy —or worse, a fraud.

And I was neither, thank you very much.

Maybe if I started a website or took out an ad, business would pick up a bit. My boyfriend Charles had already offered to refer business from the firm our way when he or one of the associates needed extra help. I'd originally rejected his offer, preferring to either succeed or fail totally on my own. Now, however, I was starting to wonder if I was being too stupid, too proud. If I could help people, do what I loved, and get paid for it, then who cared how I came about my clients?

"Can we please talk about this?" I begged my still fuming cat.

"You already know where I stand on the matter. When you decide to join me, then I'll decide to talk to you," Octo-Cat mumbled in that horrible patronizing tone I loathed.

"Fine, then you can spend our petaversary alone." Even though I knew he wasn't going to answer me, I still stormed off and slammed the door.

Of course, I hated to leave my kitty companion like that, but being together at that moment was, unfortunately, creating more problems than it was solving. Maybe with a good night's sleep, we'd be able to start this conversation fresh in the morning.

Maybe.

But until then, I just couldn't take any more fighting.

And so I set his food and water on the floor, went to retrieve his litter box, and then moved my bedding to one of the spare bedrooms so we could both have a bit of time to cool off. Once I'd settled in, I shot Charles a quick text to let him know not to come over that night and went to bed several hours earlier than I'd planned.

Happy Petaversary to me!

The next morning, I woke up feeling refreshed and much less irritated than I'd been the night before. The moment I left my temporary quarters, Paisley raced over to lick my ankles and tell me about the great adventures she'd had touring the estate with Nan.

"There are so many great places to pee! So many!" she gushed as I reached down to scratch her between her adorable oversized ears. "I love it here! It's like a paradise for dogs! I can't believe I get to live here now! I love my new life! I love you!"

I chuckled to myself while she zoomed off again. She ran in such fast, tight circles that soon she was almost completely out of breath from the exertion of it all. When Paisley slowed down and approached me again, her tongue lolled from the side of her mouth and she panted heavily, smiling up at me with unmistakable affection.

"I'm glad you like it here," I told her. "Nan and I will do everything we can to make sure you love everything about your new life. Hey, by the way, do you still want to go to the shelter with me for a quick visit today?"

"Oh, boy. Oh, boy! Oh, yes! Yes, please!" the little dog trilled, running another manic lap before returning to me once more.

I laughed again, something I could tell I'd be doing lots of now that Paisley was a part of my world. "I don't think they're open yet, but let me check their hours online and find out when they do."

Paisley followed me up the stairs and toward my bedroom—the bedroom where I just happened to know that one very crabby tabby would still be sitting by his lonesome and bemoaning his bad luck.

I stopped so abruptly that the eager Chihuahua bumped into my lower leg. "Um, I'm sorry, but Octo-Cat is going to be upset if you come in with me. Would you mind waiting outside for me? I promise to come back very soon."

The little tricolor dog plopped her butt down on the top stair and wagged her tail furiously. "I will be a good girl and wait, because that's what you said to do!"

Well, that was an entirely different response than I ever would have received from Octo-Cat. Oh, a pet owner could most assuredly get used to this. I wiped my face of the smile that had just spread from cheek to wicked cheek and quietly let myself into my cat's self-imposed prison.

"Octavius?" I called out, using his preferred name in the hopes it might earn me some sorely needed brownie points. "Are you in here?"

"Of course I'm in here, Angela," he growled from beneath the bed. "But I also smell that the dog is out there."

"Oh, Paisley? She's not coming in. I—"

Just then, the door burst open and an exuberant Paisley bounded through the door and rushed straight under the bed. "I heard you call my name. I'm a good girl. I'm coming to you!" she called as she shot past me in her renewed pursuit of her new cat roommate.

"Betrayal!" Octo-Cat cried, shooting past

me and bolting down the stairs in a whirlwind of fluff and attitude. "Betrayal of the highest order!"

Even from all the way up here, I heard his electronic cat flap beep and pull open from the foyer.

Paisley at least hadn't given chase. Instead, she stood proudly at my heels, beating a steady drum with her small black tail against the floorboards. "Did I do good, Mommy?" she asked.

I didn't have the heart to tell her no. "You did good," I hedged. "But next time, wait until I say *come*. Can you do that?"

"Yes, Mommy. I surely can do that! You're my best friend, and I love you!" With this said, she began licking my toes and didn't stop for at least three whole minutes.

Okay, fine. So maybe I was starting to find her enthusiasm *a little* annoying…

CHAPTER FOUR

Paisley and I trotted into the Glendale Animal Shelter around lunchtime. A pudgy older woman greeted us from behind a battered oak desk tucked into the corner of the entryway at the very moment we arrived.

"Welcome! Welcome!" she crooned. Then, shooting her gaze toward Paisley, she cleared her throat, dropped it a few notes, and said, "Hey, I recognize you, little dog. You aren't bringing her back. Are you? Was something wrong at home?"

Paisley scuttled back to cower behind my leg, shivering violently as I'd already come to realize was her way whenever anything either upset or excited her.

"No, of course not!" I assured them both. "We're just here for a little visit is all. Actually, is there someone I can speak with about maybe putting in some volunteer hours?"

The other woman's entire countenance lit up at this. "Oh, how lovely! Yes, yes, let me just take you back to our Community Outreach Coordinator's office so the two of you can have a little chat."

I nodded my agreement, then followed her through a set of double doors into the behind-the-scenes area of the shelter.

Paisley pranced alongside me, stopping frequently to sniff at the air or press her quivering nose to the floor. "It all smells exactly the same as it did yesterday," she mused. "Oh, can you believe it, Mommy?"

I could believe it; I could believe it very easily but chose not to say anything that might dampen the little dog's spirits. Instead, I held my tongue as our guide led us down a long, narrow room filled wall-to-wall on each side with floor-to-ceiling kennels. Sure enough, many of the dogs were housed several to a cage, just as Paisley had described the night before.

"Hey, Chihuahua! What are you doing back in this awful place?" a black Labrador mix called after us, then pushed his snout through the metal caging and whined.

"Haha. Just visiting!" Paisley cried happily. "I have two new humans. This one even talks," she added, referring to me as we continued to follow the front desk volunteer deeper and deeper into the shelter.

"It talks?" a fluffy little dog asked in a high-pitched voice. "Really?"

"*Really.* And it's a girl, so say she. That's the polite thing to do." Paisley followed up her answer by nudging my leg with her cold nose. "Hey, Mommy. Say something to our friends!"

I coughed and widened my eyes at Paisley, giving my head a subtle shake that I sincerely hoped she would understand. She was still very new to our home and didn't yet seem to understand that I couldn't exactly out my ability in front of unknown humans. I'd have to explain how everything worked once the two of us had some privacy. Hopefully, she wouldn't be too embarrassed by my unex- pected unwillingness to perform my neat human trick for the other shelter dogs.

"Here we are," our guide said brightly, rescuing me from that disappointed look on my sweet doggo's face. "You'll find Mr. Leavitt straight through that door."

"Thank you," I said, reaching out to shake the woman's hand.

"My name's Pearl," she offered with a friendly smile. "And it's my pleasure to assist. I'll be just up front, should you have any questions for me before you go. Good luck!"

I watched Pearl zoom away, somewhat confused by the fact that she'd wished me good luck. Didn't places like this always need a steady stream of volunteers?

The dogs behind us began to bark in earnest. I tried to understand what they were saying, but too many voices mixed together for me to make out any single thread. Suddenly, I felt very anxious as I raised my fist to knock on the office door before me.

"Come in," someone—presumably Mr. Leavitt—called.

I scooped Paisley into my arms, then pushed the door open. At the same exact time, the fluorescent lights overhead flickered on, off, on, and then at last off again. The long room filled with kennels fell completely dark and silent, but the small office before me had a steady stream of sunlight wafting in from the large row of windows along the back wall.

"Hello," I said shyly. "If this is a bad time, I can come back later."

The man behind the desk glanced up at me with a welcoming grin. Shockingly, he appeared to be about my age—late twenties, maybe early thirties. For some reason, I'd expected someone far older. Maybe it was the fact that the gray-haired woman I'd just met had chosen to refer to him as a Mr.

He stood and extended a hand in my direction. "You mean the lights? Nah, that happens all the time. Come on in all the way, take a seat, and tell me what I can do for you." His blue eyes shone as our hands made contact, and I swear I felt a tiny spark jump from his skin to mine.

I didn't find Mr. Leavitt particularly attractive, but there was something about him that was inescapably alluring. If this whole Community Outreach Coordinator gig fell through, I'm sure he'd have a long and prosperous career in Hollywood, D.C., or even the boardroom. He'd fit in easily anywhere charisma was valued and rewarded.

"I know this guy," Paisley said from atop my lap after I'd taken a moment to get settled in one of the padded chairs opposite Mr. Leavitt's desk. "He'd play with us sometimes. And he brought lots of people by to visit. Sometimes they would play with us, too."

I patted the dog's head instead of answering her directly. Keeping my hand there, I directed my attention back toward the only other human in the room. "As you can see, my Nan and I adopted this sweet little girl from your shelter. And, well, we're just so happy to have her that I wanted to pay it forward somewhere."

Mr. Leavitt nodded and folded his hands on the desk before him. "Pay it forward? How so?"

"Could you use any volunteers? I kind of have a way with animals." Of course that was the understatement of the year, but there was no way I was telling this guy the truth about my hidden abilities.

"That's very kind of you, Miss...?" He paused and flashed me a disarming grin.

"Russo," I offered, hating that heat was now rising to my cheeks. "Angie Russo. Hi."

He winked and leaned back in his chair, putting me at ease once more. "As I was saying, that's very kind of you for wanting to help. You probably noticed we're a bit over-crowded at the moment."

I nodded again. "Yes, that's why I thought I could help."

The lights flickered again, illuminating a small lamp on the edge of Mr. Leavitt's desk. He studied it for a moment, then frowned thoughtfully. "We're just as overcrowded with volunteers as we are animals. But I'm afraid it may not be enough."

My heart dropped straight onto the linoleum floor beneath my chair. "Is every-thing okay?" I whispered, wishing the sensitive little dog in my lap didn't have to be here for whatever came next in our conversation.

Mr. Leavitt offered an even wider smile than before. "Of course, everything's okay. At least it is for now. Just a bit of growing pains, if you will. You see, at present, we have more animals and more staff, but not more money. It makes covering all our expenses a bit tricky, but we'll manage. We always do."

Was I actually being dismissed? Had Mr. Leavitt somehow decided that my help wasn't good enough? That rankled me and suddenly made me desperate to contribute in any way I could.

"That's good to hear, but still I'd like to do something," I argued, giving him my best, most placating smile. "Would a donation be better than volunteering right now?"

He shook his head and let out a low sigh. "Oh, no, no, no. You don't have to do that. I wasn't trying to suggest——"

I chuckled as I fished around in my purse for my checkbook. Mr. Leavitt was obviously a proud man, but this was a community shelter, and I was part of said community. I owed it to the animals to make sure they had enough to eat, drink, and keep a roof over their heads. "I know you weren't, but I'm already here anyway and I want to help," I said with a shrug.

"Well, if you insist, then it would be wrong of me to say no. Thank you so much for being willing to help these wonderful animals."

Mr. Leavitt told me the information I needed to fill out my check and then accepted it with an outpouring of gratitude. "You're a good woman, Angie Russo. I can tell this little one is very lucky to have landed a place in your home," he said, scratching the mostly black Chihuahua in the center of her forehead.

And for once I didn't argue. Paisley was lucky to have us. I knew that better than ever now that I'd seen the alternative. Now, if only there was something more I could do to help the others who hadn't yet found their forever homes...

CHAPTER FIVE

After writing out the check for my donation, Mr. Leavitt showed me around the shelter and detailed how my gift would help the residents there. I left that afternoon about a thousand dollars lighter and feeling fantastic about it.

It was nice to use my money for something good. Not that it wasn't great to keep Octo-Cat stocked on all the specialty water, gourmet cat food, and new Apple technology his little kitty heart desired, but this time I was helping dozens of animals in need rather than catering to the spoiled whims of a single pampered pet.

I couldn't stop smiling the whole way home.

During that drive, Paisley and I also had a little talk about what I could and could not do in front of other people.

"So you can't talk to animals when other humans are around?" the Chihuahua summed up from her precarious perch on the passenger seat.

"Bingo," I sang with a huge smile of confirmation, then added, "Unless, of course, it's Nan, Charles, or someone else we're close to. Got it?"

"Got it," she barked, taking a quick moment to stare at me in admiration before putting her front paws up on the windowsill and basking in the fresh breeze blowing through our tiny vehicle.

Back at home, we found Nan listening to showtunes while slathering a tall layer cake with light pink buttercream. "Is that the Hamilton soundtrack?" I guessed, suppressing a laugh when I drew close enough to hear my seventy-year-old-plus grandmother rapping about the founding of our nation.

"That Lin Manuel Miranda is so talented, and so cute, too! If I were thirty-five years younger or he were thirty-five years older, I'd have a half a mind to take off half his clothes and—"

I was quick to shove an index finger in each ear so that I wouldn't have to listen to the rest of that sentence. "Nan, that's way more than I ever want to hear about that."

She chuckled and shook her head. "Hey, I may be old, but I'm not dead yet!"

I simply gave her a hug and changed the topic. "Yeah, um, right. So, uh, anyway... Has Octo-Cat come out at all today?"

Nan shrugged as she continued work on her towering bubblegum-colored confection. "Not that I've seen. How did things go at the shelter?"

A vision of all those poor caged animals sitting in their dark cages flashed through my mind, eliciting a sad sigh. "I made a donation, but I wish there was something more we could do to help. It's really crowded in there, and they even lost power while I was visiting."

"You don't say," Nan remarked, biting down on her lip and then spinning the cake before her to make sure it had been fully frosted.

"I wish I hadn't," I admitted. "What

brought you into that place to begin with? Did you know they were struggling when you went in to adopt Paisley yesterday?"

Nan took off her apron and washed her hands in the kitchen sink, then dried them on an embroidered tea towel. "I sure didn't, and the lights at least stayed on while I was there, but I did notice the fact that they had more dogs than kennels to put them in."

"So what made you decide to adopt a dog yesterday then?" I took advantage of her quiet thoughtfulness by grabbing a spoon from the drawer and snagging a spoonful of buttercream to taste.

Nan rolled her eyes playfully and followed me out toward the living room where we both claimed our favorite spots in the large sitting area filled with uncomfortable antique furniture. "Oh, I didn't decide," she revealed once we were both settled in our seats. "I just did it."

"Yup, that sounds about right," I said with a chuckle. I loved my nan dearly, but it was true that she did first and thought later—if at all. "Well, you picked a good one in Paisley. She's a real sweet girl."

"Of course I did. And of course she is," Nan clucked like a proud mother hen. "Was there ever any doubt?"

"Not at all."

We made some tea, then chatted for a bit about our plans for the week. Nan was hard at work developing new recipes for her upcoming book. It wasn't a cookbook, but rather a memoir that would be enhanced with half a dozen of her favorite custom recipes. She was also working on some kind of secret art project that she planned to convert into the book's eventual cover, but I wasn't allowed to see that until it was ready.

I had originally planned to work on rustling up some new business for Octo-Cat's and my new private investigation firm, but now it seemed I'd be spending every waking hour serving as mediator for our two pets as they learned to live in harmony.

"Would you be okay with chicken parmigiana for dinner?" Nan asked with a quick glance toward her new Apple Watch. Octo-Cat's zeal for all things iTech had spread to me and Nan, too. "We have another couple of hours yet, but it wouldn't hurt to thaw the meat a bit first."

As a proud American of half-Italian descent, I was always up for a hearty pasta dish—and everything Nan cooked tasted like Heaven to my untrained taste buds. "You know I love your chicken parmigiana," I answered without hesitation as I stretched my arms overhead and let out a happy moan in anticipation of that night's meal.

A loud crash followed by the sound of something fragile shattering on the ground sent us both scrambling to our feet.

"What was that?" Nan shrieked.

"Sounded like it came from the kitchen. C'mon."

We both rushed in and found little Paisley sniffing a broken pile of china. No, Lenox! Oh, this was not good!

"Was that one of Octo-Cat's teacups from Ethel?" I shouted, a wicked headache already brewing beneath my temples.

Nan bent down and picked up a shard. "Judging from the floral pattern around the rim, why yes. Yes, it is."

"Did you do this, Paisley?" I asked after

kneeling down to speak with the dog at her level. "Did you accidentally knock this down?"

"No way. I would never do that!" she barked, wagging her tail affectionately. "I would never break Mommy's or Nan's things."

I believed her. Not just because I knew she wanted to keep us both happy, but also because it didn't seem possible that she'd be able to jump onto the counter, push off the teacup, and then jump back to the floor without managing to hurt herself.

"Do you think Octavius broke his own cup in protest?" Nan asked, shaking her head in disappointment.

"It seems like something he might do, but he's been locked in my bedroom the whole day. Remember?"

Nan reached one hand up to scratch her head. "Are you sure you didn't leave a window open or something?"

"Pretty sure," I said, even though I couldn't really be sure of anything at the moment, at least not as far as he was concerned. "But let's go check and see if he's still in there."

"Can I come?" Paisley asked, trailing after us excitedly.

"No, he doesn't—" I began, but then quickly amended my answer. "You know what, Paze? Yes. Yes, you can come."

"Oh, joyest of joys!" the Chihuahua sang, racing up both flights of stairs as fast as her diminutive paws could carry her.

"You do realize that the cat is going to be furious with you," Nan pointed out with a naughty grin.

I shrugged. "Yeah, well, maybe I'm furious with him, too," I muttered, then took a deep breath and pushed the door open.

CHAPTER SIX

W e found Octo-Cat sitting on the corner of my bed and staring unhappily into the void. A flurry of striped hairs danced in the sunlight that filtered in through the nearby window. Just looking at the scene made me have to sneeze... and so I did.

"Why so loud?" my cat moaned in response to my *achoo*, turning toward me with a sneer on his scrunched face.

"Kitty friend!" Paisley cried as she charged toward the bed and took a giant leap upward. All that momentum wasn't enough to propel her tiny body onto the mattress, however, and she rammed into the side of the bed head-first.

Matters also weren't helped by Octo-Cat's decision to take a clawed swipe at her. "Hey, you punk! Let's get one thing straight. I am not your friend," he growled and flexed his claws, ready to take a fresh shot at the poor, misguided pup.

"That's enough, you two!" Nan hurried across the room and grabbed an animal with each arm. "Let's play nice here. After all, we're a family."

Paisley strained to reach Octo-Cat across the short distance, barking happily as she cried, "Brother, brother, brother!"

Octo-Cat mewled demonically, twisting furiously until he at last wriggled free of Nan's embrace.

As for me? I laughed and laughed hard.

Which only made my cat that much more livid with the lot of us. "Why are you bothering me?" he whined. "Go away."

"We were wondering if you knew anything about what happened in the kitchen." I studied him carefully for any glint of recognition.

If Octo-Cat knew anything, though, he didn't give it away. His face remained an unreadable mask—well, at least behind the thick layer of disdain. "What happened in the kitchen?" he asked with a yawn that smelled like two parts Fancy Feast and one part cat butt.

Oh, boy.

Maybe he actually didn't know. Maybe I was about to break his poor, aggrieved heart all over again. I thought back to the first time one of Ethel's heirloom teacups had broken, remembering his utter despair and the touching funeral that had followed.

"Are you going to tell him about the broken teacup, or should I?" Nan asked me with one raised eyebrow.

So much for putting things delicately.

"What broken teacup?" the tabby asked after a sharp gasp, struggling to speak each word with his crackly, suddenly oxygen-starved voice.

"I'm sorry," I said, and I really did mean it. "It was one of Ethel's. We were all in the living room, when—"

"Enough!" he shouted, turning on me so quickly, I took a reflexive step backward. "It was the dog, and you know it!"

I shook my head, unable to tear my eyes away from the enraged feline. "We thought that at first, but she can't reach the counters."

Paisley yelped. "I'm sorry about your teacup, brother!"

"You know, she's not that much bigger than a rat. It wouldn't be so hard to snap her neck," Octo-Cat said through gritted teeth.

"That's a very bad cat!" I yelled. "How dare you say that about your new sister?"

"She is not my family, and she never will be. Get her out of here if you know what's good for her... or for you."

Paisley let out an ear-piercing chain of shrieks and wouldn't stop.

"There, there, dear one," Nan sang softly while I glared at my cruel cat companion. It was one thing to be upset, but quite another to threaten such violence.

"Stop looking at me like that," he rasped with a weighty flick of his dark tail. "You're the one who's forcing my paw, and can't you see I'm grieving my poor, sweet teacup here?"

Nobody said anything as we all stood around my tower bedroom awkwardly. Paisley at least stopped crying, though.

"Get out of here! Go! Leave me in peace!" the distraught tabby shouted at last.

I knew he was upset, but I still couldn't believe how quickly he'd gone from simply irritated to threatening murder. It was moments like this that made me question whether my life was really better with him in it. Of course, I knew it was silly and that hunting was part of a cat's nature, but still... How could he be so cold-blooded about it all?

"Fine. We're going," I mumbled, then led Nan and Paisley from the room. "Next time we see you, I hope you'll be a bit more welcoming."

"Well, that didn't exactly go as planned," Nan whispered in my ear once we'd shut the door firmly behind our small party.

"No, it really didn't."

We trod down the stairs side by side.

Nan carried Paisley in her arms, not unlike a little baby. "What now?" she asked.

"It looks like we'll be adding to our teacup cemetery in the backyard. Other than that, I don't know. We both know he can hold a grudge for a long time, and we also know that

Paisley isn't going anywhere. I guess the only thing we can really do is wait the situation out. And maybe keep a close eye on Paisley while we do." I hadn't repeated Octo-Cat's murmured threats to Nan, and I didn't plan to, either.

Nan hummed to herself now as she thought about what we might do next. After a few moments, her face lit up and she said, "That may be the only thing we can do about this particular problem, but there's more than one way to... Oh, dear, that is a terrible expression, especially in light of current events. What I mean is there's more than one problem that needs solving."

"The shelter?" I asked, my voice cracking on the first syllable of that second word.

My grandmother nodded. "You mentioned how much they're in dire need, and I just so happen to have some extra money left over from selling the old house to Charles. Perhaps it's time I made a donation of my own."

She was right. Donating had made me feel so much better earlier that day, and at least the

shelter wanted to be helped, unlike Octo-Cat.
"Hmm. How late do they stay open? It's almost
dinner time now."

This didn't stop Nan, however. "I'll run
down now and give it a try," she said. "If
they're already closed for the day, I'll head
over again first thing in the morning."

I stopped walking and put an arm on
Nan's shoulder before she could head down
the grand staircase to the main floor. "Oh, no
you don't! There's no way I'm letting you go
on your own. Remember what happened last
time you visited the animal shelter unsu-
pervised?"

"Of course I do," Nan said with an impish
grin, lifting Paisley in her arms and giving the
little dog a kiss on her nose. "But was it really
so bad? I mean, look at this sweet girl!"

"Depends on who you ask," I said, then
motioned back toward my room with a belea-
guered sigh.

"Be right back," Nan informed me as she
turned away from the staircase and shot down
the hall to her bedroom. "I need a quick
change of costume."

When Nan joined me downstairs a few

minutes later, she was wearing a hot pink T-shirt that read *Dog Mom* across the chest. Both *O*s had been fashioned to look like paw prints.

"When did you have time to get that?" I asked with a chuckle.

"Overnight shipping, dear," was her reply as she rummaged about in the coat closet and extracted a matching pink leash for Paisley along with a...

"A spiked collar? For your five-pound Chihuahua? Really?" Now I was laughing in earnest. Just because I was never surprised by my grandmother's antics didn't mean they weren't hilarious.

Nan lowered herself to the floor and patted her lap. "Well, why not?" she mumbled while she worked on sizing the collar appropriately for Paisley's thin neck. "For all we know, the heart of a warrior beats within this tiny body."

I blew a raspberry. "Um, I can talk to her. Remember?"

"I'm a warrior!" the dog exclaimed enthusiastically, lapping up all the attention. "I'm a big, brave dog!"

I just shook my head. These two were

clearly perfect for each other, and I was so, so happy for them.

CHAPTER SEVEN

I felt like the odd one out, given that my two companions had decked themselves out in a vibrant matching shade of pink while I wore a black polka-dotted blouse and flippy yellow skirt. On the way out the door, Nan had decided to pair her T-shirt with silver sling-back kitten heels, and I'd thrown on my favorite battered combat boots. As usual, we made quite the interesting pair. Throw in the Chihuahua, and we were practically a walking fashion show—or at least a reality TV show.

We reached the shelter a few minutes before six and were greeted with a firmly locked door.

"Crud," I muttered, rattling the handle just in case.

I looked toward Nan just in time to catch her ducking around the side of the building and out of view.

"What are you doing?" I whisper-yelled, chasing after her.

"Why, looking for another way in, of course," she said, tapping a long fingernail against the window and then turning to me with a devilish smile.

"This isn't one of your spy movies, Nan. We can just come back tomorrow. No need to sneak about. Now c'mon. Let's go," I hissed as I attempted to yank her back toward the parking lot.

Nan shook me off, then raised a finger to her lips and sank to the ground, motioning for me to get down, too. "Wait. Someone's in there."

Despite my better judgement, I did as Nan instructed.

We both carefully peeked our heads over the brick ledge and peered through the window. Inside, a thin blonde woman riffled through a tall stack of papers. She muttered something to herself, but I wasn't able to make out the words.

Nan pinched me. "Will you look at that? I knew there was something fishy going on here."

Sure she did. Really, she just got lucky this time and every other time she wanted to have herself an adventure. These days, Nan was never disappointed when it came to uncovering crime and drama in our once sleepy small town.

We both watched as the blonde woman inside pulled a sheet of paper from the middle of the stack with shaking hands and pushed it through a desktop shredder. For a brief moment, she glanced up as if sensing that someone—or rather, some*ones*—was watching her, then cursed under her breath and hurried out of view.

"C'mon," Nan said, duck-walking toward the next window.

I waddled after her, and Paisley pranced after me. What a merry band of spies we made.

We didn't see the girl again until we reached the very end of the building and the room I easily remembered as Mr. Leavitt's office. Once there, the blonde pulled open the bottom left drawer of his desk and shoved the remaining papers inside, took another quick look around, and fled.

"Shoot. Is she leaving?" I asked, short of breath from the excitement of our discovery coupled with the grueling physical task of the duck-walk. "She'll see our car in the parking lot and know that someone's here."

"Ooh, you're right." Nan popped up and sprinted back toward the main entrance, beating the blonde girl by a solid thirty seconds.

If she was surprised to see us waiting outside the doors for her, she did a great job hiding it. "Oh, hello. Can I help you?" the girl asked.

"Yes, dear. Thank you," Nan answered in her over-the-top grandmother voice that she took on whenever she wanted to appear extra frail or needy. "I've come to make a donation, but I'm afraid I may not be in the right place. Is this the Glendale Community Animal Shelter?"

The blonde smiled with what appeared to

be relief. "Yes, that's us, but I'm afraid we're closed now."

"Oh, bother," Nan chirped, sounding far too upbeat given the words she'd just spoken. "Well, that's what I get for nodding off during my stories."

"Aww, it's okay," the girl said, shooting Nan a placating smile. "We open again tomorrow at eight. Or, if you prefer, I can take your check now and make sure it gets into the right hands tomorrow."

"Oh, bless you, dear," Nan said with a gracious smile. "That would be wonderful. Now what's your name? I want to make sure I can mention to my followers on the Facebook how helpful you were to me this evening."

"I'm Trish," the girl introduced herself with a laugh. "And thank you. We can use all the volunteers and all the donations we can get."

"Well, Trish." Nan extracted her check-book from her purse. "It isn't much, seeing as I'm on a fixed income, but I hope it gives you the help you need."

"No amount is too small. Believe me. I don't have an extra two pennies to rub together, which is why I donate my time instead," Trish explained as she shifted her weight from one foot to the other.

"They're very lucky to have you," I said, when Nan didn't.

Trish and I watched in silence as Nan wrote out a check for one hundred dollars and tore it from her checkbook with a flourish.

"On behalf of the animals, thank you very, very much for your generosity," the girl said, holding Nan's donation close to her heart.

"Oh, it was nothing," Nan responded with a dismissive wave. "I just wish it could have been more."

"Every small donation makes a huge difference." Trish folded the check in half and stuck it in her front pocket. "I'll be sure this gets added to our coffers tomorrow. Good night, and thank you again!"

We returned her goodbye, waited for Paisley to take a quick potty break, then headed back to the car.

"Who was that?" the little dog asked. "I've never seen her before."

"Trish," I explained. "She's one of the

volunteers. Are you sure you haven't seen her before? She's obviously not new if she's in charge of closing up."

"Nope, never," Paisley answered without the slightest hesitation. "She was really pretty, though. I like her."

"Wait," I said with a creeping grin as I thought of the early days with Octo-Cat back when he was simply upset about me providing him with the wrong brand of bottled water as opposed to threatening to murder a Chihuahua. "Do you maybe not recognize her because all humans look the same?"

Paisley's long pink tongue lolled from her mouth as she panted in amusement. "Why would you say that? Humans don't look the same at all, and you smell very different, too! Nope. I definitely would have remembered seeing—and smelling—her before."

I quickly caught Nan up on the dog's and my little side conversation.

"Hmm," she said with a dramatic huff. "That's a bit odd."

"It is," I agreed. "What do you think Trish was doing in the shelter all by herself? Does she actually volunteer there, or no? And what did she secretly shred?"

"Good questions," Nan answered as she navigated the roads that would lead us back toward our home. "One thing's for sure, I'll be keeping a close watch on my bank account to see where that check actually ends up."

I nodded to show my agreement. "Smart."

"Maybe tomorrow night we can go back and try to break in," she added with a completely serious expression on her wrinkled face.

"Nan," I scolded. "We're trying to stop someone else from breaking the law, not break it ourselves."

"Well, you're no fun," she groused.

Maybe I wasn't fun compared to my wild grandmother, but one of us had to be the level-headed one in this investigation.

And with Octo-Cat out of commission, apparently that job would fall to me.

CHAPTER EIGHT

W e returned home to find my boyfriend Charles waiting on the front porch. As soon as I parked the car, I ran up the short set of steps and straight into his outstretched arms.

"What are you doing here?" I asked after a quick peck hello.

"Well, I missed seeing you yesterday when the petaversary celebration got cancelled. And when we talked earlier today, you just seemed so down. You know I had to come by and cheer up my best girl." His eyes held mine as he spoke, making me feel weak in the knees. Even though we'd been dating for a few weeks now, I still couldn't get over the fact that we were finally together. I'd crushed on him for so long, and now? He was my honest-to-goodness boyfriend—and a really great one at that.

Once I had my strength back, I pulled away and studied his handsome features. "Your best girl?" I asked with a giggle. "That sounds an awful lot like something Nan would say."

"Okay. Fine," he confessed with a breathy laugh. "So maybe she did call and put me up to it, but the important thing is that I'm here now and I have something special planned for us tonight."

I hugged Charles tight and pushed my face into his chest in an attempt to hide my nervous expression. I was still pretty new to this whole relationship thing and terrified I'd do something to mess it up at any minute. We were especially tricky, too, given that we'd become such good friends before ever getting romantically involved.

Because of our unusual timeline, I feared we were dangerously close to the "I love you" stage even though we'd only been dating for a little less than a month. I also feared the "Will you marry me?" stage might quickly follow once the first three little words were out of the bag. And as much as I adored Charles, the thought of becoming somebody's wife—of living with anyone other than Nan—made me break out in goose bumps and a cold sweat all at once.

One day at a time, I reminded myself as I so often did. The now was very good indeed, and I needed to take some time to enjoy these early puppy love days of my first real adult relationship.

Swallowing down the last dregs of my anxiety, I asked, "Am I allowed to know what you have planned, or is it another one of your famous surprises?"

Charles kissed my forehead, then released me from his embrace. "This time, I'll tell you," he answered with a smirk. "But next time, I'm keeping whatever I plan for us a surprise until the last possible moment."

I nodded, still focused on the now and eager to find out what we'd be doing that night.

Charles put both arms around my waist and pulled me close. "There's a new day spa that just opened up on the edge of Dewdrop

Springs, and they're running a special on couple's massages. I figured we could go check it out. What do you say?"

"I say, *sign me up for that!*" I squealed and gave a happy little leap into the air. I'd never had a massage before, but I'd heard good things—mostly from my grandmother. Truth be told, the whole idea made me a bit nervous, but I appreciated Charles's gesture too much to let him in on any of the hesitation or worry swirling through my mind.

"Bye, dear," Nan called after us as Charles led me to his waiting car. "Don't do anything I wouldn't do!"

I laughed so hard at that I almost choked. Nan would do just about anything with hardly a moment's thought first, definitely not the model for chaste behavior. Then again, maybe that was the point she was trying to make here.

"Thanks for getting me out of there," I told my boyfriend as he backed us out of the long driveway.

"Any time," he promised me with a smile that made me want to kiss him right then and there. "Is Octo-Cat still pouting about the new arrival?"

I sucked air in through my teeth. "That would be putting it mildly."

He chuckled at this. "Remember Yo-Yo?"

Ahh, Yo-Yo the Yorkie, the only witness to his owners' double murder. That was the case where Charles and I had first become good friends, even though the whole thing started with him blackmailing me and threatening to expose my secret to the world.

"Of course I remember Yo-Yo," I said with a smug grin. "I also remember how Octo-Cat never quite got used to him for that whole time they were together."

"That was only the better part of a week. Paisley will be around for the rest of his life. Even he can't wage his silent protest for that long."

"Oh, ye of little faith," I quipped, then rolled my eyes for good measure.

We drove for another half hour before reaching our destination. The swanky new spa was part of a run-down strip mall, which didn't inspire much confidence on my part. Once we pushed through the doors, however, we were greeted with a beautiful office space, painted in a tranquil green with a large stone fountain bubbling near the welcome desk. Soft classical music piped through hidden speakers, and the woman waiting to greet us wore all white from head to toe.

Her red hair shone even in the dim lighting, and her pale skin appeared flawless to my untrained eye. "Welcome to Serenity," she said melodically. "How may we improve your world today?"

I fought back any number of sarcastic comments that were teetering right on the edge of my tongue and gave this would-be world-improver a tight-lipped smile.

Charles, however, seemed far more in his element. Perhaps because he'd grown up in California. He forged right ahead in the direction of the woman and the desk, grabbing one of my hands and tugging me along as he went. "We're here for a seven o'clock couples massage," he informed her.

"Ahh, last spot of the day. Excellent." She paused for an unnaturally long time before adding, "You'll rest well tonight."

Another awkward pause.

Charles and I glanced at each other questioningly, then back toward the woman.

"Stone is just finishing up with his previous appointment, if you'll please have a seat." She floated out from behind the desk and guided us toward a pair of giant exercise balls set around a small area rug.

"Um, thanks." I sank awkwardly onto the dark green ball, leaving the tan one for Charles.

The welcome desk lady smiled at us for slightly longer than was comfortable, then let herself into the back room, leaving Charles and me by ourselves. Well, Serenity was certainly a strange place, if the greeter was any indication. This made me more nervous than I'd been before. Of course, Nan would like this whole dog and pony show. She liked everything, the weirder the better. Me? I preferred to stick to what I already knew and loved.

"You don't think Stone's that guy's real name?" Charles asked, making a funny face.

I was about to ask him the exact same thing, but instead I hit him playfully and giggled. "It all contributes to the *ambience.*" I over pronounced that word so much it sounded like it belonged to another language. French, maybe.

"It's all part of improving our world," he added with a quiet chuckle as he bumped his giant exercise ball seat into mine.

I rolled back to gain some momentum, then nudged his even harder than he'd bumped mine. A flirtatious game of bumper balls followed, each of us making up the rules as we went along.

We didn't even notice at first when the attendant returned—not until she cleared her throat loudly and stared unforgiving daggers our way.

"Stone is ready for you now," she alerted us, forcing a smile for Charles's benefit, I would guess.

Just then, the door to the back swung open and a lithe, blonde figure emerged.

"Trish?" I asked, unable to believe I'd managed to run into the shelter volunteer twice within the span of about an hour—especially considering the distance we'd all had to travel to arrive at the shopping center from Glendale.

Trish blinked over at me, then smiled. "Oh, you came with your mom today to make a donation. Right?" she asked sweetly, so sweetly that it seemed very, very fake.

"My nan, actually, but—yeah—that was me." I smiled graciously to show I meant her no harm. "What are you doing here?"

"N-n-nothing," came Trish's shaky reply. "Just headed home."

And before I could ask anything else, she flew out the door.

Well, so much for making small talk.

CHAPTER NINE

I'm not exactly sure what I'd expected from Stone, but it wasn't the new-age Irish lumberjack who greeted us a short while later.

Though he wore all white like the front desk attendant, he had a completely different vibe. A gigantic toothy smile peeked out from behind his thick red beard. "Good evening," he said as he pushed through the room, his long arms dangling as he moved toward the cabinets that lined the back wall. On his way, he turned up the music track; the soothing sounds of an exotic stringed instrument filled the room, adding to the otherworldliness of this whole experience.

"I'll return in five minutes to begin your

massages." Stone handed us each a fluffy white robe, then left to give me and Charles the chance to change into them privately.

Whoa. He'd hardly exchanged five words with us before instructing Charles and me to take off our clothes! It's not that I was a prude, but I'd always been modest about my body.

I'd never even been naked in front of Charles before, but thankfully he was a gentleman about the whole thing. He turned his back to me and promised not to look until I told him it was okay. Still, I tore off my clothes and yanked on that thick robe with record speed. The unfamiliar garment seemed to swallow me whole, but at least it was comfortable against my bare skin.

"You can turn around now," I called sheepishly. In fact, I felt like a sheep, too, as I stood swaddled in that overly fluffy cotton robe.

And if I was a sheep, then Charles was definitely that cartoon wolf, sizing me up. He let out a low whistle and remarked, "You look extra cuddle-able right about now." Closing the short distance between us, he then wrapped his arms around me and swayed to the meditation music in a ridiculously misguided romantic gesture.

"I'm naked under here," I whispered, embarrassment setting in.

He just laughed and continued to dance with me until a soft knock sounded on the door.

"Come in," Charles called as I clutched my robe even more tightly.

Stone had returned with the front desk attendant in tow. "This is my colleague, Harmony. We'll be massaging you together. Please make yourselves comfortable."

Charles widened his eyes playfully and rubbed his hands together, then made his way to the first of the leather massage tables, slowly lowering himself and lining his face up perfectly with the hole at the top.

"Now you, Angela," Harmony coaxed. Her voice sounded different than it had upfront. Perhaps it was the different acoustics, or maybe she truly had a different voice for working the front desk versus working on a client. Whatever the case, it seemed mighty weird to me.

Apparently sensing my discomfort, Charles reached out and touched my arm as I passed. He was such a good boyfriend, and so much more cultured than me.

I took in a deep breath, vowing to give this whole experience a fair chance before deciding it wasn't for me. After shooting quick smiles to Stone and Harmony, I at last positioned myself on the table—far less gracefully than Charles had, but at least the deed was done.

"Lavender for relaxation," Harmony said, spraying something all around the room.

"Our own proprietary blend," Stone added fondly.

The two took turns speaking to us in quiet, even-tempered voices. Their words blended together perfectly, and I imagined this whole opener had been rehearsed many times to get it just right.

When they had finished, Harmony placed a soft, warm hand on my neck and began to tug gently on my robe.

My heart sped to an uneven gallop. Weren't massages supposed to be calming? Because my anxiety had officially been kicked into overdrive here. "Can I keep the robe on?" I mumbled, hoping it was loud enough for her to hear me.

"No," she said in a voice that brooked no argument, lowering the robe farther and farther until at last she stopped at my hips.

"It's okay, Ange," Charles said from beside me. "It's normal to be nervous the first time. Just keep talking until you relax."

The first time? Had Charles done this before? Had he done it with his ex, Breanne? Yuck, I sure hoped not.

Still, by the time my masseuse had begun to rub oil into my upper back, I'd decided to take Charles's advice. At least talking would make the time go by a bit faster.

"Nice place you've got here," I mused. "Of course, I can only see the floor right now, but the stuff I saw when coming inside was nice, too. Haha."

"Relax," Harmony cooed, sweeping her hands gently along my spine. "Relax."

That did not help me relax.

"So, you guys are new around here? Right? What made you decide to set up shop in Dewdrop Springs? And why is it called

Serenity? And are your names really Harmony and Stone?"

"Relax," Harmony said again, a sharp edge working its way into her previously calm voice. What would happen if I didn't relax? Would they call the whole thing off? I didn't want to do that to Charles, especially knowing how hard he worked as the only partner at Glendale's most infamous law firm.

"Sorry, I'm just nervous." I took several slow, shaky breaths, trying to match my breathing to Harmony's, hoping that's what would ultimately help me get into the right headspace for this experience.

"You'll enjoy our work more if you let your tension go," Stone suggested rather unhelpfully.

"This is her first time," Charles explained. "Can we all just talk a little to help her ease in?"

"We won't be going over the allotted appointment time," Harmony warned. Each time she spoke, her voice lost some of that ethereal quality. I wouldn't be surprised if she worked her way up to screaming at me before long.

"We don't need to," Charles was quick to respond. "But she's not going to have a good experience if we don't help her relax."

"Fine," Harmony spat while Stone just chuckled good-naturedly. Of course, I got the ice queen masseur, but I suppose it was better than having the unknown man's hands all over me while I lay there exposed and helpless.

"We're called Serenity because that's the aura we try to create for all who pass through our doors," Stone said.

"What about Trish?" I asked, unable to help myself as I thought back to the startling encounter with the lithe blonde. "She didn't seem very serene when she ran out of here in a hurry."

"We don't discuss other clients," Harmony said, giving me a little pinch as she did.

"Clients? Was she here to get a massage?" I asked innocently.

"Yes," Stone answered definitively. "Yes, she was. And don't worry about her. Her experience definitely wasn't typical. She at least left us with less stress than she brought in with her."

Harmony let out a frustrated groan but said nothing more.

"Why is she so stressed?" I asked.

Although I certainly hadn't expected an answer, Stone provided one anyway. "Because the city cut funding to the animal shelter, and they're having a rough time over there."

"Stone," Harmony hissed. "Remember our code of ethics, please!"

Everyone fell silent for a few minutes.

"Hey," Stone said, forgetting to use his soothing meditation voice. Rather than sounding irritated though, he came across more like a friend. "You know what helps me when I'm feeling nervous? I like to list all the things I'm grateful for. Let's all take turns as we focus on the positives in our life. I'll go first. I'm grateful for being able to do what I love for a living."

"Me, too," Charles piped up.

"Me, too," I said. "Well, sort of. I haven't been doing much of it lately, but—"

"No explanations," Harmony snapped. "Just state your thought, release it, and move on."

"Fine," I snapped back. "Then I guess I'm grateful for my cat."

But was I grateful for this experience? Certainly not.

Maybe next time Charles would let me plan date night.

CHAPTER TEN

"Did you enjoy your massage?" Charles asked after Harmony and Stone left us to change out of our spa robes and back into our street clothes.

"Yes," I said definitively, hoping that he would believe me. I appreciated the gesture but didn't find the actual act of getting touched all over by a stranger very relaxing at all. I'd much rather pet Octo-Cat or Paisley until all my troubles melted away. Or get in a few snuggles with my boyfriend. Or go on a sugar binge with Nan.

Basically anything other than being poked and prodded by an angry person fake-named Harmony.

"You're such a bad liar," Charles said with a chuckle. "And even though I couldn't see you, I could still tell your wheels were spinning that whole time. You were thinking about the shelter. Weren't you?"

Okay, he knew me eerily well, but I guess that was just part of his charm. "Don't you think it's weird that city hall would cut the shelter's funding when it's already struggling?"

"Maybe the shelter isn't the only thing struggling," Charles suggested. "This past year we've had a pretty high murder per capita. It could be that people are moving away, houses are sitting empty, and the local government has less money to spend overall."

"Maybe," I agreed half-heartedly. His logic made good sense, but my gut was telling me something else was to blame here. "But I don't think that's it. It seems like something fishy is going on with the shelter in particular."

Charles played right along. He, too, had learned to trust my instincts, and he never made me feel bad about needing to investigate —or obsessively discuss—a hunch. "And you think that woman we saw... Trish... is at the center of it all?"

"Of course I do." I accidentally turned around before Charles had finished getting dressed and caught an eye full of his bare legs and chest. "Oops, sorry."

"Don't worry about it. I'm not nearly as shy as you are."

I waited for that tell-tale sound of pants zipping up before turning around again.

When I did, Charles greeted me with a grim expression. "But I can't help worrying about you. Are you going to at least be careful about inserting yourself into a potentially dangerous situation this time?"

I shook my head and let out a sarcastic huff. "I'm always careful."

Charles laughed so hard he had to cough. "Yeah, we both know that's not true, so let's try again. Can you at least be more cautious than you usually are?"

"Fine," I acquiesced and let him wrap his arms around me. "Although you know I no longer work for Longfellow and Associates, which means you're not my boss anymore, either."

"Yeah, but you mean more than ever to

me now. You think I'm only warning you off because I'm your boss? That hurts."

"No, I'm sorry. You're right. Any other demands, oh great and powerful boyfriend?"

"Now that you mention it." He placed a kiss on my forehead first, then my nose, and finally finished up with a lingering kiss on my mouth. "I do have one tiny request."

Even before Charles said anything more, I already knew I'd grant him any wish he wanted. I was a big pile of cotton fluff in his hands. *Literally.*

"Let me swing by city hall to see what information I can gather about the budget cuts. Once I do that, you're free to investigate to your heart's content."

"Fair enough." I pulled his face back down to mine and gave him another enthusiastic kiss.

"What was that for?" he asked with a smile once we'd pulled apart.

"For trying to make me feel better, and then actually doing it."

"So, you mean I shelled out for this fancy couple's thing when all I had to do was wave my lawyer card around a little?"

We both chuckled and then kissed again. Even if I kissed Charles every day for the rest of my life, I doubted I'd ever grow sick of it, sick of him.

Still, we had things to do, so I reluctantly pushed him away. "Now turn around and face the wall so I can get dressed in peace," I instructed, happy to put this whole experience behind me and get back to the real world where people went by their given names and spoke in their actual voices.

Buh-bye, Serenity.

Hello, mystery at the shelter.

I returned home to what could only be described as a war zone. Nan wore pink camo sweatpants to go with her pink *Dog Mom* shirt, and even her adorable sidekick Paisley had undergone a costume change. The shaking ball of sleek fur now wore a skull and crossbones tank top with a glittery pink bow affixed to one side of the skull.

Oh, brother.

In the dining room, a giant map of the

Blueberry Bay region took up most of our large table. Nan had also brought out a fresh piece of poster board and a rainbow array of all her favorite Sharpies.

"What's going on here?" I asked, not entirely sure I wanted to know the answer.

Noticing my arrival at last, Nan marched straight across the room and put a hand on each of my shoulders. "The check was cashed," she informed me, eyes flashing with glee.

I frowned. This seemed like a ridiculously over-the-top way to celebrate a check being cashed. Of course, my head was all fuzzy from Harmony's massage, so maybe my synapses were still slow to fire.

"And you turned our house into a war room, because…?" I asked, anyway.

Nan pointed toward the desktop computer she kept set up in the far corner of the living room for her occasional use and said, "Remember how you taught me to pay all my bills online?"

"*Yessss,*" I answered slowly, not sure I liked where this was going. It was one thing for me to take risks for a case, but I hated the thought of ever putting Nan in harm's way.

"Look at this." She thrust a piece of computer paper at my chest.

Although the image was grainy, I could clearly make out the scan of Nan's check from earlier that day, along with the sloppy signature and the stamp that read First Bank of Blueberry Bay.

"Check out the address," Nan urged me with an eager smile.

"Dewdrop Springs, *huh,*" I read aloud. "But why would the Glendale Animal Shelter be cashing checks in Dewdrop Springs?"

"That's what I was hoping to learn from you. You were just over there, after all." She grabbed the paper back and waited for me to explain everything.

I didn't have the answers she was looking for, but I did have a bit of information that could help us get there. It was my turn to make a big reveal, and I relished it. "Now that you mention it, Charles and I did run into Trish at the massage place. Do you think she's the one who cashed the check?"

We both studied the messy scrawl of the

signature, but it was impossible to decipher without knowing Trish's last name.

"Weird," I said at last.

"Definitely weird," Nan agreed with a nod.

"So what is all this about then?" I motioned around at the giant mess that had exploded in our normally pristine home during my brief absence.

"It's easier for me to think with all my supplies close at hand," Nan answered with a shrug.

This made me chuckle. "And what have you thought of?"

"That we definitely need to be investigating that shelter more for a start," she said without a second's hesitation.

"Yeah, I kind of have the same feeling, too. Ooh, let me catch you up on what I learned while I was out."

"Excellent, but first, tea," Nan declared.

She scurried toward the kitchen with a plucky Paisley in tow, then let out a sharp gasp. "Oh, dear. I think we've had another attack!"

I raced after her only to find a pair of coffee mugs shattered against the hard floor.

What in the heck?

Who was breaking all our things?

And how had Nan not heard all this racket from the next room over?

Sigh.

It seemed that we now had more than one mystery to solve.

CHAPTER ELEVEN

Despite my niggling dislike of Harmony, even I had to admit she'd gotten one thing very right: I slept like a log that night. It could have been the massage, or it could have been the fact that I'd decided to stop tiptoeing around my angry cat and had actually gone to sleep in my own bed when the time came.

I hadn't laid eyes on Octo-Cat before tucking myself in but knew he must still be somewhere in the tower bedroom. Not that I cared all that much at the moment. Honestly, I was so done with this tantrum of his. He could either learn to live with Paisley or he could make himself a prisoner in my bedroom until the very last day of his very last life.

I hoped it wouldn't come to that, but he'd made it quite clear that he wasn't willing to negotiate when it came to our new doggie family member.

Beyond exhausted, I didn't rouse that morning until my angrily ringing cell phone forced me out of bed.

"Ugh, what time is it?" I groaned in the general direction of the phone instead of saying hello outright.

Charles laughed on the other end of the line. "Wake up, Sleeping Beauty. Your prince charming has some news!"

"Sleeping Beauty has Prince Phillip," I corrected, wiping the sleep from my eyes.

"And you have Prince Charles. Oh, *hmm*, maybe not." He chuckled to himself, but I was still too groggy to join in.

"Anyway, I've got news," Charles continued. "And it's almost ten o'clock by the way, you should really get up and greet the day."

I groaned again, which only made my boyfriend laugh harder. "What's your news?" I asked, searching my nightstand for the gummy multivitamin I took each morning.

"Well, I started my day at city hall as

promised. You can really learn a lot when you know the right people, I might add." He sounded quite proud of himself. Did this mean he had found something good? Something that would help Nan and I figure out what in the heck was going on with that shelter?

"And what did you learn today?" I asked with a smirk before popping the sugary vitamins into my mouth.

He sucked air in through his teeth, then explained, "That the animal shelter funding hasn't been cut like Stone said. In fact, it's increased year over year beyond inflation."

I yawned and tried my best to refocus. It was way too early for words like *inflation*. "Which means?" I asked, hating how stupid I must sound to Charles's educated ear. Granted, my seven associate degrees were nothing to shake a stick at, but they still weren't nearly as impressive as his one law degree.

Charles took a deep breath, then revealed, "It means that if the shelter has a money problem, it's not due to lack of funding."

"Do you think someone's stealing?" I

asked, unable to think of any other possibility given the way that evidence had been stacking up the past couple of days.

"Stealing from a business—or in this case a nonprofit—is called *embezzlement*. And, yes, it does seem like that might be a possibility here." The fact that Charles had shifted into full-on attorney mode told me that whatever was going on, it was very, very illegal. I sincerely hoped the culprit would not only be caught, but also punished to the fullest extent of the law.

Rage flew through my veins, waking me up better than any form of caffeine ever could. "But it's not just money," I argued. "It's these animals' lives! They're already three to a cage… What happens if the shelter has to be shut down?"

"Maybe another shelter would take them in." Charles's whispered words betrayed his true beliefs. He felt just as hopeless as I did in this situation, and it didn't do anyone any good skirting around the issue.

"Or maybe they'd all be turned loose on the streets. Or worse, eu-eu-euthanized." I shuddered at that last word. It represented one of the most awful things I could imagine. Those poor sweet animals.

"That's not going to happen," Charles assured me. His voice came out stronger now, surer.

"But how? How can you know that for a fact?" Hot tears stung at my eyes, but I refused to let them fall. I needed to stay angry. Angry got things done.

"Because I know you, and I know you would never let that happen," my boyfriend told me.

"I gotta go," I mumbled into the phone, already halfway to my closet and ready to throw some clothes on in a hurry.

"I know you do," Charles said, and I could hear the smile in his words. "Stay safe and call me if you need anything. Got it?"

"Got it," I said, then pressed to end the call.

Never had I been so determined to solve a case—and to solve it quickly. Dozens of lives depended on it.

By the time I'd clambered down the stairs in my hastily assembled outfit, Nan was already dressed and waiting for me at the front door. "Finally," she said with a huff. "Ms. Paisley and I have been waiting all morning."

"Hi, Mommy!" Paisley cheered, wiggling her butt in merriment. "We're going for a car ride!"

"To the shelter?" I asked, just to be sure.

"To the shelter!" Nan called in a rallying battle cry, then flung the front door open so that the three of us could march into battle.

This time, we took Nan's little red sports car instead of my old clunker. "We want them to know we have money and that we aren't afraid to use it," Nan offered as an explanation.

"Is that the whole plan?" I wondered aloud. Once again, I was worried that Nan had chosen to view complex problems far too simplistically. The world inside my grand-mother's head and the world as it actually was didn't always line up perfectly. God bless her.

Nan shot me a warning look as she twisted the key in the ignition. "Of course not!"

"Then fill me in already."

"You'll see when we get there," she said with a wink and then pushed down hard on the gas pedal.

Whatever happened next, I was ready for it.

Although I hoped Trish wouldn't be there this morning; otherwise, Nan's whole feeble retiree on a fixed income act from yesterday evening would fall apart the very moment she was spotted pulling up to the shelter in an expensive sports car. It seemed unlikely we'd run into Trish, given that Paisley had sworn up and down that she'd never seen the mysterious volunteer once in her entire life.

But, still, I had to wonder...

We got there quickly, thanks to Nan's penchant for driving at least ten miles above the speed limit wherever she went. And it wasn't Trish, but rather Pearl—the kindly, older volunteer I'd met on my own yesterday —who greeted us upon our arrival.

"Back so soon?" she asked with a warm grin. It took me a moment to realize that her smile wasn't intended for me, but rather Nan.

"You know me," my grandmother crooned. "I just can't stay away."

Turning to her side, Nan motioned toward me but continued to address Pearl. "This is my granddaughter, Angie, and of course you already know Ms. Paisley."

Paisley barked in acknowledgement.

I simply nodded and forced a grin.

"Hello, Angie," Pearl said as she regarded me with a blank expression. Did she really not remember meeting me only yesterday? "Now, what can I do for you, Nan?"

I found it downright hilarious that this old woman was calling my grandmother *Nan* of all things, but I at least managed to keep a straight face throughout their exchange.

Nan brought a hand to her heart and sighed. "I can't stop thinking about these poor animals and the trouble you folks are having."

"Oh, don't worry about us," Pearl answered with a sad shake of her head. "We'll find a way. We always do."

"Surely, there must be something I can do," Nan pressed.

Pearl rose to her feet and placed a placating hand on Nan's arm. "I promise we're doing all we can. It's just the funding's been cut, and we're still trying to find a way to work within our new budgetary constraints."

Nan chewed her lip. Whether she was honestly disheartened or just putting on a good show, even I couldn't say for sure.

"I understand, I do," she mumbled, "but —hey, I've got it!"

Pearl and I both waited to hear what Nan would say next, and she, of course, kept us waiting to heighten the anticipation.

"Well? What's your big idea then?" Pearl prodded.

Nan flashed a toothy grin before revealing her grand idea. "What if I were to put on a big fundraiser to help save the shelter?"

"We're not really at the point of needing saving, but your heart is in the right place. Tell you what, I'll take you to Mr. Leavitt, so the two—" She paused and glanced back toward me with a nervous smile. "—I mean, the three of you, can discuss this in private."

Nan gave a single affirmative nod. "Thank you, Pearl. That would be lovely."

The other woman smiled and led us toward the door that led deeper into the shelter. As we followed her back through the long room of kennels, Nan reached out and squeezed my hand. I was still flying blind here as far as her plan went, but at least we seemed to be making forward progress.

I only hoped that would continue...

CHAPTER TWELVE

M r. Leavitt welcomed Nan, Paisley, and me into his office with huge smiles for everyone. And unlike Pearl, *he* remembered meeting me the day before.

"Welcome back, Angie," he said, clapping a hand on my shoulder as I passed through the door and into his office. "I'm starting to suspect you may be our own personal angel here at the Glendale Community Animal Shelter. You not only wrote us a generous donation of your own, but you came back the very next day with a new donor. Please, both of you, come right in."

That's right. I had given him a check. Had that really been less than twenty-four hours ago? And was it cashed at the same time and place as Nan's donation? So much had happened in that short span, I'd forgotten to look into it.

"I'm going to do so much more than write a check," Nan told him, lowering herself into one of the chairs opposite Mr. Leavitt's desk. "I'm going to put together a fundraiser so lots of people can write checks. How about that?"

Mr. Leavitt's eyes grew wide with the promise of a large cash infusion. "Well, now, I love the sound of that," he chortled. "Now, tell me. How can I offer you my assistance?"

"I'm glad you asked," Nan chortled right back. "I won't need much, I promise, but I *am* going to need some time to get a feel for the facility and the animals who live here. That will help me make sure I'm planning the right type of fundraiser. After all, why throw a bake sale when what you truly need is a gala?"

"Too true, too true," Mr. Leavitt said, bobbing his head as his eyes grew wider still. "It would be my privilege to give you a tour of our facilities. If you'll just give me a few moments to finish a few things first, I'll—"

"Actually," Nan interrupted. "I'd much

rather walk around by myself, if you don't mind. I'm sure you understand. I need to feel the place out, not listen to a speech about its history." She crossed her legs and sat straighter, spoke more commandingly.

And Mr. Leavitt immediately fell under her spell. "Oh, of course. If you need anything—"

"Then I know who to come and find. Thank you," Nan finished for him, then rose back to her feet and walked out without waiting for me and Paisley to follow.

I had to power walk to catch up. "Now what?" I whisper-yelled as she strode confidently through the kennels.

"Now we're going to chat with some of the animals and see if they know anything." *We.* Yeah, right. It was my neck that was on the line here.

"Nan, what if someone catches us?" I asked fearfully, silently adding, *What if they overhear our suspicions and decide to hurt us to keep us quiet?* It had happened before. It could most assuredly happen again. One thing I'd learned well during all my months of sleuthing is that criminals hated being caught. Obviously.

Nan didn't seem worried in the slightest, however. "I'll stand guard, and if anyone catches us, you can just pretend you were talking to me or to Paisley," she explained with a no-nonsense expression. "But be quick, I doubt we're going to get another opportunity like this one."

Paisley, right.

I sure missed having Octo-Cat as the Watson to my Sherlock.

The little dog was nice enough, but I still didn't know how much Paisley actually understood about the mystery we'd uncovered.

Guess it was time to find out.

"Hey there, Paisley," I cooed, lifting the dog into my arms. "Wanna help me with a little game?"

"A game!" the Chihuahua barked. "Like fetch? Or keep-away? Or, or chase the cat? Yes! I love those games!"

"Not exactly," I hedged, biting my lip for a moment as I thought. "This game is called *Detective*. We play by trying to figure out a secret."

Paisley rearranged her face so that one of her lower canines overlapped her upper lip.

She looked so stinking cute as she said, "I don't have any secrets. Can I still play?"

"Of course you can," I assured the tiny black dog. "In fact, we already know what the secret is, but we don't know who it belongs to. Do you think you can help me figure that out?"

"I will try my best, Mommy!" Paisley promised, shaking with newfound glee.

"Great, that's the spirit!" I gave the doggo a wet kiss on her forehead followed by an enthusiastic scratch between the ears. "Okay, the secret is that someone is stealing money from the shelter, but we don't know who is doing it."

"What's money?" Paisley asked, quirking her head to the side in interest.

"Forget the money," I said, backtracking fast. "What I meant to say is that someone at the shelter is being very bad, and it's up to us to figure out who."

"Hmm," Paisley said, her ears twitching like miniature satellite receptors. "I bet it was a cat!" she shouted after a few moments' thought. "When these things happen, it's usually a cat."

This made me laugh. "Actually, I'm pretty sure a human is to blame this time."

The little dog whimpered. "But all the humans here are so nice," she argued. "They feed us and walk us and play with us and help us find homes. Nobody is bad, and definitely not *very* bad." She actually shuddered at the thought.

Oh, dear sweet Paisley.

She really did see the best in everyone. Even the cat at home who'd threatened to kill her and the people at the shelter who were stealing resources from the animals in need. As much as I wanted her help, I doubted I'd get her to see the truth even if it happened to come out and stare straight into her soul.

"Okay, tell you what," I said, changing tactics. "You keep Nan company, and I'll talk to some of the other animals and see what they have to say. Sound good?"

"Okay, Mommy!" Her tail wagged so fast it became a blur. Oh, to be that happy!

I set Paisley down, and she immediately bounded over to Nan and stretched her tiny paws in the air, begging to be picked up and cuddled. "Keep an eye out," I mumbled, then jogged to the last cage at the very farthest end of the room. Might as well be organized about my investigation.

An enormous wrinkly dog stared up at me with sad eyes. At his side sat a much smaller hound mix whose sole focus was biting and chewing one of his hind feet.

"Hey, there," I cooed, absolutely hating the air of sorrow around this place. These two at least seemed older and wiser than Paisley. Perhaps that would be to my benefit. "My name is Angie, and I was hoping you could help me. A very bad human is stealing from the shelter. Any idea who that could be?"

"All the humans here are nice," the big dog informed me with zero hesitation.

"Yeah," the hound added around a mouthful of foot. "If anyone is being bad around here, it's probably a cat."

"Oh, yes. Thanks for your help," I said, forcing a smile. We'd only just begun and already it was abundantly clear that I wouldn't be able to learn much from the dogs here. Still, I spoke to several more before finally giving up and heading to speak with the cats as suggested.

The cat area of the shelter was much smaller and offered no privacy, which wasn't a problem since every set of kitty eyes and ears fixed on me from the very moment I entered.

"Hi," I said nervously, even though I fancied myself a cat person. I loved Octo-Cat when he wasn't being needlessly cruel and dramatic, but the thought of twenty of him in one place scared the living daylights out of me. "My name is Angie, and I'm trying to find a very bad human who works at the shelter. Do you know—?"

"Darling," a flat-faced fluffball drawled, cutting off my question at the quick. "Look around. All humans are bad."

"They'd descend into chaos without us cats around to keep an eye on things," an orange tabby with an angry face insisted.

No wonder cats and dogs disliked each other so much. They were as different as two creatures could come. Still, at least they didn't blindly trust everyone's motives. Maybe they'd be able to offer some kind of clue if I asked my questions right.

I cleared my throat and tried again. "Is there one human that's worse than the rest?

Maybe someone who is stealing money from the shelter?"

"That's like asking if there's one blade of grass that's greener than the rest," the flat-faced cat spoke again. "There are just so many of them, and they're all green besides."

The other caged felines meowed their agreement, and I officially gave up on finding any leads via the shelter animals.

It was time to do things a little differently.

Unfortunately, I didn't have any idea how.

CHAPTER THIRTEEN

Octo-Cat sat waiting for us in the living room when Nan and I returned home. I'd left the bedroom door open before we headed out just in case he might want a change of scenery, but I hadn't exactly expected him to take advantage of it.

Luckily, Paisley was already tucked securely into Nan's arms, so she couldn't be tempted to make a run for the ornery feline. Couldn't Octo-Cat see how much she already loved him? How much she wanted to be his friend?

Judging by the tabby's furrowed brow and tense posture, that was a hard no.

"Well, look what the cat dragged out," I

quipped, part relieved to see him and part worried about what he might demand next.

"Hardy har har," he said dryly and then, "I see you're still playing house with that imposter."

Well, as it turned out, we'd made no progress at all. "You saw right. Now don't you think it's time for you to stop your pouting and rejoin the living?"

Had I made a mistake by kowtowing to his demands about the Fancy Feast and the Evian and the exquisite manor house? It had been easy to do regarding mere things, but now another life was involved. I refused to send Paisley back to that overcrowded shelter, especially when its future was so uncertain.

I knew it wouldn't be so easy, but still my heart ached when Octo-Cat responded with, "Bad things happen when good cats remain silent."

"But that's exactly what you're doing!" I argued. "Giving me the silent treatment. Haven't you had enough?"

"Haven't *you* had enough?" he shot back in a deep, ominous voice. Something told me there was no right answer here.

"Mr. Octopus Cat," Paisley squeaked, drawing both of our attention to her big black eyes and tiny pink mouth. "I know you don't like me, but I promise I'll do anything to make things right. I want to be friends."

"Aww, how could you say no to this face?" I cooed, scratching Paisley under her tiny, quivering chin.

Her whole body squirmed in response, and Nan had to make quick adjustments to avoid dropping her.

"Easily," Octo-Cat spat, unmoved by the show of love. "Very easily, indeed."

"Are they finally playing nice?" Nan asked, a hopeful sparkle in her eyes.

"Um, not exactly," I answered with a sigh. "But this is progress, nonetheless."

"Say, dog," my cat lisped, rising to all four paws. "Will you really do anything to make me happy?"

"Oh, yes!" Paisley cried, her shaking thus renewed. "Yes, I will do anything!"

I waited in silence for the big reveal. Would Octo-Cat's demand be one we could meet? I'd do almost anything to bring peace to our divided house.

The cat's large, amber eyes narrowed, and he spoke very, very slowly. "Then run far, far away and don't ever come back."

The Chihuahua whimpered, which made our evil feline overlord laugh. "Do I really have to, Mommy?" Paisley asked, a pathetic whine lacing each of her words.

Oh, that cat! He made me so angry sometimes!

"No, of course not. He's just being mean!" I scowled at my unruly pet, but he didn't look the least big apologetic.

"Hey, I know what I want." Octo-Cat flicked his tail in one direction and then the other. "And also what I don't want. The dog needs to go."

"Hush up, Octo-Cat. You've been outvoted," Nan said, even though she couldn't understand any part of the conversation other than mine.

Paisley wriggled and licked Nan's hands, whether to derive comfort or to agree with what had been said in her defense, I couldn't be sure.

"Unbelievable," my cat mumbled as he hopped to the floor and skulked out of view. A

few moments later, we heard his electronic cat flap lift open and admit him into the outside world.

"And stay out until you've had an attitude adjustment!" I shouted after him.

"Don't worry about him, you sweet girl." Nan kissed the Chihuahua's head and then set her on the floor. "Let's go make ourselves some lunch. Huh?"

We all moved to the kitchen, where Nan took out three chicken breasts to grill on the stovetop and I began working on the fixings for a Caesar salad. "I'm making one for Paisley, too," she explained with a grin.

Oh, the little dog would definitely love that.

We'd almost finished our lunch preparations when a loud crash sounded from the foyer. I glanced toward my feet and found that Paisley had left us some time ago.

"Why does everything keep breaking around here?" Nan grumbled as she removed her pan from the burner and marched out to locate the source of the disturbance.

I spotted the mess before she did. One of Ethel Fulton's antique Tiffany lamps lay in pieces by the entryway. A priceless heirloom. *Great.*

Paisley stood beside the mess, howling. "I'm so sorry," she cried. "I don't know how it happened. I was just minding my own business, and—crash!"

"It's okay, sweetie. We know you didn't mean to," I coaxed as Nan began to sweep up the mess.

"Unbelievable," Octo-Cat mumbled and then ran up the grand staircase, presumably back to his self-imposed prison in my bedroom tower.

Funny, I hadn't heard the electronic pet door buzz open even though we were standing directly beside it.

"Can you watch Paisley for me this afternoon?" Nan asked once the three of us had finished our mid-day meal. "I'd bring her with me, but I have a lot of errands to run and don't want her to get lost underfoot."

"Sure," I answered absentmindedly while logging into the bank's mobile app on my phone. I had to click around a bit to find exactly what I was looking for. When I did, I handed the phone to Nan and asked, "Hey, is this address the same as the one on the check you had cashed?"

Nan studied the tiny screen for a moment, then handed the phone back my way and rummaged around her desk until she found the printout she'd made the night before. "The very same," she said, holding the paper beside the phone screen so the two of us could compare.

I glanced between them a few more times, feeling more and more confident that we'd made a match with each new look. "The signature's a little different on this one, but it looks like it belongs to the same person. I think maybe it starts with a *D* or an *O*. Hard to say for sure."

"But that's not how you spell Trish," Nan said with a sigh.

"No, it's not," I agreed, feeling more confused than ever as I logged out of the app and set my cell phone back on the table.

"I'll think on it while I'm out," my grandmother promised.

"Where are you going, by the way?" I'd only half paid attention when she said she was leaving and was curious now that she'd brought it up again.

"To begin work on the charity fundraiser for the shelter, of course. I've decided to go with a gala. That will bring all the key players out better than any bake sale or car wash ever could."

"Good thinking." Or was it? I hated contradicting her, but had she really thought this whole thing through before deciding to jump into action?

"Nan, a gala takes a lot of prep work, though. What if it's too late for the shelter by the time you've finished the planning?"

She waved her hand dismissively. "Stop being such a negative Nancy. You know better than to doubt your nan. Now, you two be good. I'll be back in time to rustle up some dinner. *Ciao.*"

And just like that, she was into her shoes and out the door. Man, she moved fast. I often felt like a slouch next to my fit and active grand-mother. Maybe one day I'd actually do some-thing about it—but today was not that day.

"What would you like to do this after-noon?" I asked, searching the floor for Paisley. Normally, she clung to the closest human like a bur, but at the moment, I couldn't spot her anywhere.

"Paisley!" I called. "C'mere, girl."

"I don't wanna," came the muffled reply.

It took a few minutes, but I finally found her hiding under our antique Victorian loveseat. "Why so sad, sweetie pie?" I sat down on the hard, uncomfortable floor and waited for her to show herself.

"The cat doesn't like me," she sniffed while remaining firmly in place beneath the old couch.

"Oh, don't worry about him. He doesn't really like anyone."

"He doesn't like me *a lot*, though. And at the shelter, I couldn't help you win Detective. And now Nan left and didn't want to take me with her. What if she never comes back?"

The poor dear! I hated that she felt this

way and that there was very little I could do about it.

"Paze, please don't cry. You did a great job helping with Detective, and—hey—the game's not over yet. We still have time to win. And I promise Nan will come back just as soon as she finishes her errands. We all love you very much."

"Even Octopus Cat?" she asked, raising her head slightly.

"Even Octo-Cat," I assured her with a chuckle. "He just doesn't know it yet."

CHAPTER FOURTEEN

Seeing as both Paisley and I could use a change of scenery, I leashed her up and drove us downtown to enjoy a bit of window-shopping.

"Have you been here before?" I asked my doggie companion as the two of us strolled down the narrow sidewalks that flanked the commercial heart of our small seaside town.

"Nope," Paisley answered, then stopped to squat beside a young tree that had just begun to change colors for the fall. "But I like it very much. So many excellent smells!"

Although I was sure our definition of *excellent* varied substantially, I smiled and nodded my agreement. Paisley was happy again, and that's what mattered most.

"Which smell is your favorite?" I asked conversationally.

"Oh, definitely all the pee!" she squealed, happier than a pig in number two as she enjoyed the apparently intoxicating aroma of number one.

I didn't ask any more questions after that. Instead, the two of us continued on our way, stopping frequently to allow the Chihuahua to sniff anything that caught her fancy.

"Oh, hello there, Angie!" Mr. Gable, the owner of the nearby jewelry store, called from the spot where he was idling with a steaming mug of coffee. The old man had become something of an institution here in Glendale, and it was no wonder he'd recently been voted head of the downtown council.

"Hello, Mr. Gable," I called, quickening my pace to join him.

"And who might this little fella be?" The smiling, white-haired man carefully lowered himself to the ground and let Paisley sniff his hands. His coffee, too.

"This is Paisley," I announced proudly. "Nan's and my newest addition."

He laughed good-naturedly. "Oh, I bet the cat doesn't much care for that."

"You bet right," I answered with a laugh. Hopefully, Mr. Gable's well-meaning comment wouldn't turn the dog into a nervous, shaking mess all over again.

In the end, she appeared too taken by the kindness of this new friend to worry about the unkindness of the hostile feline back home.

Mr. Gable and I chatted amiably for a few minutes about the upcoming holiday spectacular. We were a good three months off, but it was widely known that the downtown businesses started planning on December 26 of the previous year. The yearly festival got bigger and grander with each run, and I couldn't wait to see how it would look this Christmas.

Mr. Gable, however, refused to give anything away. "It's better as a surprise," he promised with a Santa-like wink.

Just as I was about to press a little harder for details, an unexpected movement down the street caught my eye. Mind you, we were in downtown Glendale, which meant lots of people, dogs, and vehicles came and went— even in the middle of the day.

Somehow, though, I knew the sudden pale blur wasn't a part of all that. I guess you could say my kitty sense was tingling.

Paisley felt it, too, because she nudged my foot with her nose and said, "It's that nice lady we smelled the other day. Remember at the shelter?"

And she was right. Suspicious Trish had made yet another appearance in my life, and I wanted to know why.

"Well, nice chatting," I told Mr. Gable with a brief wave goodbye. "We'll see you soon."

I picked up Paisley, even though I knew she'd probably rather walk, and hurried back in the direction from which we'd come. I needed her close so that I could whisper to her about what would happen next.

"We have to be very, very quiet," I told the little dog, channeling my inner Elmer Fudd. We weren't hunting wabbits, though, we were stalking suspects—and that was way more dangerous.

"If we can stay quiet and hidden long enough, I think we might just win Detective," I promised with a quick grin.

Paisley gasped but said nothing in response. Good dog.

Trish cut through an alley, and I raced faster to catch up, making sure I remained far enough behind to avoid letting her spot me. She stopped in a parking lot and stood, waiting.

Paisley and I hid ourselves behind a nearby dumpster. Neither of us spoke a word.

Then I spotted it, a giant, beat-up Cadillac crunching onto the gravel lot. The driver was most definitely male, but I couldn't make out much more than his wispy frame and deep voice. He and Trish spoke for a few minutes and then he hopped out of the car and popped the trunk open.

Inside, the spacious trunk was filled to the brim with pet supplies, still in their packaging. If the mysterious man was here to make a donation to the shelter, he was sure acting shifty about it.

I didn't have long to puzzle over this, because the very next thing I knew, Trish had pulled a wad of bills from her front pocket and handed it to the driver.

And that was more than enough to make me finally spring to action. First, I grabbed my phone and zoomed in on the license plate, so I'd have it for later. Then I placed a call to my good friend Officer Bouchard and told him he needed to come down straight away.

"Did we win Detective?" Paisley asked, staring up at me with glistening dark eyes.

"Yeah, I think we did," I told her, offering an enthusiastic petting for the job well done. "But we need to be quiet just a little longer before we can know for sure."

We watched as Trish and the man had some kind of argument, and then he drove off with both the cash and the pet supplies. Trish groaned and stalked back toward the alleyway, where Paisley and I still stood crouched behind the dumpster.

Uh-oh.

I needed to think fast, so I set my dog on the ground and cried, "Oh my gosh, Paisley! There you are! I've been looking everywhere for you!"

"Yes, I'm right here, Mommy!" the little dog barked, not quite catching on to the ruse.

Trish walked by us without so much as a nod of recognition, so I called after her. "Hey, Trish. Is that you? Three times in less than twenty-four hours! What are the chances?"

She grimaced but stopped moving at least. "I'm sorry, I can't really hang around and talk. Nice to see you, though." Without waiting for my response, she quickened her pace again and continued down the alley.

Oh, no you don't. You're not getting away that easily.

She must have had an awful lot on her mind, because Paisley and I easily trailed her without her discovering us. She moved fast, and I wished for the second time that day that I was in better shape. Somehow I managed to keep up, though, as Trish led us to a second parking lot on the other side of downtown Glendale where the same man from before sat waiting in his idling car.

"Bingo," I whispered, then sent a quick text to Officer Bouchard to let him know we'd relocated to the north parking lot.

Trish unlocked a dirty white sedan and

popped its trunk, then together she and the man began to move the contents of his vehicle into hers. They'd managed to clear about half of the goods by the time Officer Bouchard's police cruiser joined us on the scene.

My excitement mounted. My cop friend had made it on time, and now this was it. Somebody was going to be in big trouble.

CHAPTER FIFTEEN

The man pushed his trunk closed, but not fast enough to escape the notice of the officer who'd just arrived on the scene.

I took this as my cue to come out of hiding. This time there hadn't been a dumpster, so I'd had to resort to pressing myself flat against the brick wall in the alley. I strode into the parking lot with confidence I didn't quite feel—and wouldn't until I knew for sure we'd caught the crook who was embezzling money from the animal shelter.

Officer Bouchard saw me first and reached his hand overhead in a wave.

Both Trish and her accomplice spun in my direction, and the moment she spotted me, her eyes filled with disdain. "You followed me!" she cried.

"Now, now," Officer Bouchard said peace-ably. "We don't want any more trouble than is already here. Go ahead and open up the trunk, young man."

I was close enough now to make out our mystery man's features. He was tall and lanky with light skin and even lighter hair. As far as I knew, I'd never seen him before in my entire life.

"Hey, wait just a minute," Trish argued, pointing a shaky finger my way. "She followed me. Isn't stalking, like, illegal?"

"Not *like* illegal. It is illegal, but something tells me there's something even more illegal in that there trunk, and that Ms. Russo was just doing her civic duty by calling it in and keeping an eye on you until I could show up to officially handle things. Now open that trunk."

Trish's accomplice did as he was told, once again revealing the trunk filled with brand-new pet supplies.

"And that one, too, please." The cop pointed to Trish's filthy white car and waited until she complied with his order.

"Well, well, well," Officer Bouchard said with a chuckle. "These wouldn't happen to be the pet supplies a shop in Dewdrop Springs reported missing earlier today." He raised an eyebrow and glanced at the younger blond man. "Or would they?"

"Whatever, man. I'm just the go-between. She's the mastermind."

If he was sorry, he didn't look it. I had to wonder if perhaps this man was from out of town, if he'd thought no one would notice some missing pet supplies. Apparently he hadn't counted on the fact that everyone notices everything in a small town like ours.

Trish stamped her foot on the ground. "How dare you try to pin this all on me!"

"Enough bickering," the officer warned. "Who's stealing and why?"

"I didn't steal anything," Trish ground out. "I bought these supplies fair and square."

The policeman crossed his arms and stared down the bridge of his nose at both culprits. "Well, *I'm* not buying it, little miss. Why buy pet supplies from the back of some guy's trunk when it's just as easy to go to the store and purchase them there? You know, like you're supposed to?"

"He was giving them to us at a discount. We needed the savings. The shelter isn't doing so good, and... And I was just trying to help the animals!"

"Let's go," Officer Bouchard said, uncrossing his arms and making a sweeping gesture toward his waiting car. "I'd love to hear more about this down at the station. And you're both invited."

Trish scowled at me as Officer Bouchard nudged her toward the police cruiser. He hadn't cuffed either her or the man with the trunk full of stolen goods, but he had called for backup to come clear the scene while he dealt with the suspects.

"Thanks, Russo," he said, returning to my side. "But I've gotta ask, what made you decide to follow her?"

I quickly caught him up on Nan's and my suspicions, ending with a dramatic, "And she doesn't even actually work there. At least I think she doesn't."

"Oh, you and your nan. One of these days we should formally hire you to work for the county. I can promise you this, though. We're going to find out what's going on at that shelter. Stealing from animals in need is a level of despicable I don't like seeing in our town. Both of my cats were adopted from that very shelter, come to think of it."

"Officer Bouchard," I said with a grin, bumping my shoulder into his. "I had no idea you were a cat person."

He put his tough cop face back on and sniffed. "Yeah, well, don't let word get around. I already get more than my fair share of guff from the other guys at the station."

"Your secret's safe with me," I promised, loving this new detail about him. I was a cat person, too, after all. Well, most days at least.

"I've got things from here," he informed me. "Now go try to enjoy the rest of your day." The cop gave me a firm nod, which I took to mean I was formally dismissed from the investigation. Hopefully, the county would be able to finish strong from here, which meant Nan and I could focus on our little mystery at home. Namely, why so many fragile things kept breaking.

"Did we win?" Paisley asked as the two of us headed back down the alleyway.

"Yes, the bad guys have been caught, and all is right with the world again," I assured her. I missed having Octo-Cat's assistance, but Paisley hadn't been such a bad crime-solving companion this time around. With time, she could learn. The three of us could work together... That is, if Octo-Cat ever got over his ridiculous aversion to dogs.

Then Paisley asked a question I hadn't been expecting. "They seemed really nice to me. How do you know that they're bad?"

"Because they did bad things," I answered simply, honestly.

She appeared to think about this for a moment, then asked, "So if I do bad things, am I bad?"

"No, that's not the same."

"Why not?" Paisley's ears lowered, giving her an even more puppy-ish appearance than usual.

Clearly, I had a choice to make. I could let the Chihuahua keep believing the best of everyone, or I could destroy her innocence by explaining how mean the world could be sometimes.

At the end of the day, I liked my new dog daughter exactly as she was, so I said, "You know what, Paze? You're right. It was just a game. Now let's go see if Nan's back home yet, huh?"

"Oh, yes! We've been apart forever! I miss her so much!" Paisley cried, our deeper conversation about ethics and morals all but forgotten.

Maybe it was time for me to go back to Blueberry Bay Community College and grab an eighth associate degree. This time in Philosophy. Next time Paisley hit me over the head with questions like this, I wanted to be ready.

I sent Nan a quick text to let her know we were on our way home and to ask if she could meet us there, then I let my sweet little dog take all the time she needed enjoying her scenic scenting tour through downtown.

And she made sure to tell me each time she found a new one, too. Especially if it was pee.

Dogs were so weird.

CHAPTER SIXTEEN

Nan beat me and Paisley home, which was probably a good thing considering what we found when we got there.

"There's poop everywhere!" I cried with a disgusted groan.

"You should have seen this place before I started cleaning up." Nan squirted another shot of all-natural cleaner on the rug and gave the smelly stain a good, solid scrub.

"This is gross." I crossed my arms and surveyed the damage with a frown. "Do you even think it will come all the way out of the area rug? This was original with the house."

Nan paused and studied me with a furrowed brow. "What worries me more is that one of the animals has to be very sick to make such a huge mess."

Paisley kneaded her front paws against my leg and begged for me to pick her up. "It wasn't me," she said in a soft, sad voice. "Honest."

"It couldn't have been Paisley," I relayed to Nan, setting the dog back down and then slipping on a pair of thick yellow rubber gloves to help clean up the mess. "She was with me the whole time you were out, and this mess wasn't here when we left for our walk earlier."

"Even still." Nan moved to another spot on the carpet and scrubbed vigorously. "We should take both of them to the vet. Maybe she'll have some tips on helping them adjust to their new living arrangements."

"But Paisley isn't the problem," I reminded her. "Octo-Cat is just being stubborn."

"Well, we have to do something." Nan frowned at the spot and sprayed some more cleaner. "What if Octavius isn't just being mean for meanness's sake? What if he's seriously ill?"

That thought hadn't occurred to me

before, but now that Nan had mentioned the possibility, it was all I could think about. As much as Octo-Cat had irritated me the last few days, he was still my best friend and I couldn't picture life without him.

"I grabbed a doodie sample before I started cleaning up, so the doc will have that to test. I've already called and let her know we'll be coming in shortly."

"Then let's go," I said, peeling my gloves off, then picking my purse back up from the coffee table. "We can clean the rest of this up after."

Nan followed suit. "I'll wash up real quick, then grab the sample and get Paisley and myself settled in your car. You go on upstairs and get Octavius."

Right.

My cat didn't like car rides under the best of circumstances, but now that he was sick and expected to take today's ride with his sworn nemesis, it would be downright impossible to convince him to come willingly.

I briefly considered my options as I jogged upstairs to collect him. I could try asking nicely, but that would alert him to my intentions and ultimately make catching him so much harder after he refused to come peacefully. I could also try forcing him into his walking harness, but I knew well enough from experience that this was more of a two-person job. That left only one option, and it was the one I knew he would hate most of all: the cat carrier.

I hadn't ever used it before, but the very fact I kept it in the house for emergencies was a constant source of discontent for Octo-Cat.

Well, at least we'd finally have the chance to make use of the thing.

I grabbed the greatly despised carrier from storage and blew off the thin coat of dust that had settled on top of its plastic shell. Climbing the stairs to my tower just as quietly as I could, I let myself into the bedroom while attempting to hide the bulky carrier behind me.

It didn't work.

"I see you," my cat hissed from beneath the bed. "And whatever you want from me, the answer is an emphatic no."

"I'm sorry about this," I answered, pulling my bedframe away from the wall with a series of grunts and tugs. "But I can't let you waste away in here any longer, especially seeing as you're sick."

Octo-Cat moved with the bed, remaining dead center, which made him incredibly difficult to reach. Even when I dropped to my belly and extended my arms at full length, my fingertips just barely brushed the tip of his tail.

"I'm not going, and you can't make me."

Ugh. Why did he have to be so difficult?

I didn't want to manhandle him given his upset belly, but bribing him to come out wasn't exactly a possibility either. Some things about our relationship were easier because of our ability to talk to each other, while others were infinitely more difficult. This was one of those infinitely more difficult things.

Think, Angie. Think!

And then I had an idea that I was about ninety percent certain would work. I moved to my desk and grabbed the small keychain I kept in my top drawer in case of an emergency, then I gathered my comforter from the bed and bundled it up in my arms. Holding tight to the wad of blanket with one hand, I used the other to activate the keychain light.

And the red dot came to life on the carpet before me.

One of our past acquaintances had used the power of the red dot to trick two unwitting cats into doing something very bad. At the time, Octo-Cat had explained to me that while most cats logically knew the dot was just a result of a laser pointer, they also couldn't resist pouncing whenever that little sucker made an appearance.

That's precisely what I was counting on now.

The dot danced when I wiggled my hand —and when I flicked my wrist, it jerked wildly to the side.

This sent Octo-Cat shooting out from beneath the bed at lightning speed.

Thankfully, I was just fast enough to toss the blanket on top of him as an impromptu net, and—gotcha!

He was captured and spitting mad about it, too. "I will never forget this betrayal, Angela. Never. Not in all my lives."

"I'm sorry," I muttered again, picking up the blanket with him in it and then releasing him into the plastic carrier.

There.

I'd done it, and by some miracle neither of us had managed to get hurt in the process.

"Don't worry," I cooed softly even though my breathing was now labored from this whole debacle. "We're going to get you all patched up at the vet. You'll be feeling like yourself in no time at all."

"But I'm not sick," he argued before coughing up a hairball right inside the carrier.

CHAPTER SEVENTEEN

O ur usual veterinarian wasn't at the office that day, but the newest member of her practice was able to squeeze us in for an emergency visit. From the looks of her smooth skin and perky posture, Dr. Britt Lowe had only finished veterinary school quite recently. If her supposed lack of experience caused me to worry, though, her friendly demeanor and knowledgeable speech instantly put me back at ease.

"On the phone you said one of the animals—probably the cat—is experiencing a bout of diarrhea. Anything else to add?" she asked looking from her chart to the place where Nan and I sat in twin bucket seats inside the cramped exam room.

Octo-Cat growled in the carrier that I'd set on the floor beside me.

"Oh, he does not sound happy," Dr. Lowe added with a frown. "Do you mind if we take him out while we talk? When animals get this worked up, it's best to get things over with as quickly as possible. Poor guy."

"Sure, if that's how you want to do it." I lifted the carrier onto the metal table between us, then allowed the vet to open the latch.

Octo-Cat immediately tried to make a run for it, but she caught him without much trouble and used her hold on the angry feline to examine his eyes and teeth.

"There's a good man," she said soothingly. My guess is the only reason she managed to avoid getting bit was the fact she hadn't referred to him as kitty. Something about the vet's skilled hands calmed him a bit. Perhaps he knew that she was on his side in all this. That she just wanted him to be happy and feel better.

Not that I didn't want those same things, but...

Dr. Lowe set him on the table, keeping one hand on Octo-Cat's back as she motioned for me to join her. "Now hold on tight to him. Most cats don't like this next part."

Before I could ask any questions, she stuck a thermometer up his backside.

Octo-Cat's eyes widened to a comical size, but he didn't make a single peep until she'd finished. "I feel so violated," he moaned.

"You can let him go now," the vet informed me, and as soon as I did, Octo-Cat hurled himself back in the carrier he had loathed only minutes before.

Dr. Lowe frowned. "His temperature is normal, and he seems very healthy. Are you sure it wasn't the dog who made the mess?"

"We're sure," Nan piped up. "But I did bring a sample in case it helps." She handed Paisley off to me and then fished around in the disposable shopping bag she'd brought with her until she found the triple-bagged fecal sample.

"Oh, dear," the veterinarian said with a laugh. "I think I see the problem."

"Don't you need to test it first?" I asked,

unable to see what was so funny about this disgusting situation.

"No, I don't think I do. That's not cat feces. It's not dog, either."

"I told you I'm not sick," Octo-Cat pouted from inside his carrier.

"Then what is it?" I asked, completely at a loss for ideas.

Dr. Lowe held the sample up to the light, and we all stared at it as she explained, "This definitely came from a wild animal. Judging from the size, I'd guess a raccoon."

Raccoon!

Now it all finally came into focus. Octo-Cat had been able to be in two places at once by employing the help of his biggest fan, the raccoon that lived under our porch. His name was Pringle, and he worshipped the ground my spoiled cat walked on.

"Could you maybe give us a moment?" Nan asked politely. It seemed she too had figured out exactly who was to blame for all the strange happenings around our house as of late.

"Of course." Dr. Lowe nodded, then let herself out through the back door.

Once we were alone again, I bent forward so I could look Octo-Cat straight in the eye. "Please tell me you didn't really hire your raccoon fanboy to frame Paisley for your bad behavior."

"I didn't," he said, but even he didn't seem to believe it.

Placing both hands on my hips, I narrowed my gaze and waited.

My cat came to the edge of the carrier and laid back down with a sigh. "First off, hire would imply that I paid him. He did it for free. Secondly, it's not my bad behavior. I didn't do anything."

"But you're the mastermind," I pointed out.

And then it occurred to me... "Why would you break your own teacup?"

He let out another heavy sigh. "Pringle isn't the best at following instructions. He grabbed the wrong cup by accident. Believe me, I'm quite upset over it. We haven't even had the funeral yet."

"How could we have when you've been either hiding or scheming all day?" I asked, shaking my head with fury.

"You make a decent point," Octo-Cat conceded. "But my point also remains. I don't want the dog to live with us."

"Why not?" I demanded.

"I don't like dogs," he groused.

Oh, no. He was not pulling this one again. If he really hated Paisley, then he needed to be able to tell me why. I doubted he could, and I was more than ready to call him on that bluff.

"But why don't you like her, specifically?" I asked, raising an eyebrow in suspicion.

"Because she's a dog. Duh."

"Mommy, can I try talking to him?" Paisley asked from my arms. She was so light I'd almost forgotten I was holding her.

At the Chihuahua's request, I gently set her on the exam table so she and Octo-Cat could sit face-to-face. It struck me then that she'd never once had this kind of opportunity with him. The cat had always yelled, complained, and then run away to hide. But would he actually have a conversation with her now that he was stuck inside this tiny room?

"Hello, Octopus Cat," Paisley began with a reverential dip of her head.

"My name is not Octopus Cat," the tabby growled. For a moment I worried that he would take another swipe at her, but he kept his claws under control.

Brave little Paisley either didn't know that she was talking to an animal on edge or she was ready for whatever consequences she reaped as a result of this conversation. "Oh, then it seems I might have misheard," she said, blinking slowly. "What is your name?"

"My name—and you better remember this, because I'm only going to say it once—is Octavius Maxwell Ricardo Edmund Frederick Fulton Russo, Esq. P.I." He rolled each of the Rs as if doing so were required to pronounce the monstrous moniker properly.

I put a hand over my mouth to keep from laughing. Every time Octo-Cat gave out his full name, he added something to it. I was starting to doubt he'd ever been given any middle names at all.

"It's very nice to meet you, Octavius Maxwell Ricardo Edmund Frederick Fulton Russo, Esq. P.I." The Chihuahua said, carefully mimicking the cat's pronunciation and causing my mouth to fall open in shock. I'd known this cat for over a year and still didn't have all his names memorized. Had the young dog really picked the entire train wreck of a name up after hearing it just once?

"My name is Paisley Lee," she informed him with another slight bow of her head. "When Nan adopted me, she gave me her last name, so I guess we aren't really brother and sister. I'm sorry if my calling you brother upset you. I know now that I was wrong."

"It's all right," Octo-Cat mumbled, obviously charmed by the little dog's impeccable manners even though he most certainly wished that he wasn't.

"I really would like us to be friends, but if you don't want that, I understand," Paisley squeaked. Tears lined each of her large black eyes, but she continued on bravely. "I will try my very best not to chase you anymore or to make you unhappy in any way, but please can I stay? This is my family now, too."

"I guess that would be okay with me," Octo-Cat said and then retreated deeper into his carrier.

The conversation had reached its natural

end, and somehow everyone had managed to survive.

We really were going to be all right, after all.

CHAPTER EIGHTEEN

True to his half-hearted words, Octo-Cat quit hiding in my bedroom non-stop and started to rethread his life with ours. He didn't even leave the room when Paisley entered anymore, which I considered a huge step in the right direction.

Paisley adopted the practice of not speaking to him unless he spoke first, and occasionally he actually would initiate a brief conversation with her.

Several days passed, each better than the last.

Now that we'd solved the mystery of the broken household items and both pets were on their way toward forming a lasting friendship, my thoughts returned to Trish.

The county police had found enough evidence to charge her with Class C Theft after a bank teller in Dewdrop Springs identified Trish as the person who had cashed Nan's and my donation checks the week before. She'd then used that money to purchase several hundred dollars in stolen pet supplies. Together, the stolen cash and goods tallied up to just over one-thousand dollars, which marked her actions as a felony in our great state of Maine. She was still awaiting her trial at the moment, but Charles had informed me that the punishment could be both a hefty fine and possible jail time.

I still remembered how kind she had been to Nan and me outside the shelter when we first met her and how she'd mentioned not having much money herself. But was she really the type to steal from animals in order to line her own pockets? And if so, then why did she use the cashed checks to purchase supplies for them?

Something wasn't sitting right about the whole situation, but I couldn't quite figure out what. At a loss for answers, I let my questions about Trish and the embezzlement at the animal shelter simmer at the back of my mind as I worked on building a website for Octo-Cat's and my new P.I. company. Eventually we'd have customers, and I wanted to be ready to wow them when they finally came calling.

Maybe someday soon, he'd agree to let Paisley join the investigative team. I, for one, knew the little dog would love the chance to play—and win—Detective again.

That morning, Paisley decided to celebrate her new kind of sort of friendship with Octo-Cat by bringing him a present. We'd just finished tea when the little dog skittered in through the electronic pet door. Her collar was now outfitted with a coded chip, too, which meant she could come and go as she pleased —just like her new hero, Octo-Cat.

Our raccoon friend Pringle, on the other hand, had been given a massive lecture and a warning that we were to never, ever see him in the house again, no matter what Octo-Cat said was or wasn't okay.

"Hey, girl," Nan called when she saw the dog's small, dark form traipse through the foyer. "What have you got there?"

Sure enough, Paisley had something large stuffed inside her mouth, which she brought straight to Octo-Cat and laid at his paws, her tail a waggly blur of joy. Thank goodness, the tabby had been laying on the floor rather than the couch, because the gift in question was a very large and slightly bloody mouse.

Dead, of course.

Octo-Cat studied the corpse before him, then looked back up at Paisley. His eyes softened as he asked, "For me?"

She blinked and shivered and wagged. "Cats like mice. Right?"

I think Octo-Cat surprised us all with his genuinely large smile.

"Yes, and the deader the better. Good job, kiddo."

The sight made me want to throw up, but I felt too happy to let my roiling stomach stand in the way of this important bonding moment. "You know cats are supposed to be the ones to catch mice," I informed them both.

"That's old-fashioned thinking," Octo-Cat protested. "Besides, she caught this mouse for me, which kind of means I'm the one who did it, anyway."

Paisley beat her tail against the ground, hanging on every word that spilled forth from Octo-Cat's lips.

"Nice try," I said with a sarcastic chuckle. "But you can't just take credit for someone else's..." My words trailed off, and I looked toward Nan.

"What is it, dear?" she asked, then took another sip of tea.

"Trish," I said, thinking back to how sure I had been that we'd caught the bad guy and put the mystery at the shelter to rest. Too sure. The evidence was too neatly wrapped up in a nice little bow.

"What about her?" Nan said as the animals continued to share their gross bonding moment separate from us.

"Well, what if she wasn't the one stealing money? What if someone else was doing it but let her take the fall?"

"You think she was framed?"

Nan's even tone bothered me. Did she really not believe that I was on to something here?

"I'm not sure, but it's a possibility. All the evidence was too neatly stacked against her," I explained, using the same wild hand gestures my Italian-American father often used while trying to make a point. "Either she's a terrible criminal, or she's not one at all."

"Interesting," Nan said and dipped a cream-filled cookie into her tea.

"Think about it. She was the one sneaking around after closing time. She's the one who shredded that paper. I saw her in Dewdrop Springs the same night our checks were cashed there, and she wasn't exactly subtle about buying those stolen pet supplies in broad daylight."

"But didn't she also tell those massage people that the shelter had its funding cut?" Nan pointed out as she stared deep into her teacup. "Charles checked and said that wasn't true."

"Yes—but oh! When we went back to the shelter the next day, that old woman, Pearl, also said the funding had been cut."

"Who you calling old?" Nan's voice finally picked up some passion. "She's at least fifteen years younger than me."

"Sorry, Nan," I muttered. "But how well do you know Pearl? She seemed to know you quite well but couldn't remember me."

"She was in my community art class over the summer. Remember that?" She finished her tea and set the cup and saucer on the coffee table, then leaned back in her chair.

"Would you say she's the type to steal money from the animal shelter and then lie about it to others?"

"Certainly not. She was always on and on about her volunteer work with the shelter. She loves those animals as if they were her own."

"Then who else would have the means, opportunity, and motive to take that money?"

"Trish did mention being short on cash when we bumped into her outside the shelter," Nan reasoned. "Then again, money is its own motive, whether you have it or not."

"It has to be somebody inside. Somebody with access to the finances." I picked at a hangnail as I thought, a bad habit I'd thought I'd seen the last of. Apparently not.

"And somebody who could weave a narra-tive about funding cuts that others would willingly believe." Nan nodded and bit her lip. What a pair we made.

We both thought a little while longer, and then suddenly we had it.

"Mr. Leavitt!" we cried in unison, turning toward each other in excitement.

"Oh, he is going down," Nan promised the universe.

"We need to get him to confess somehow," I said, because apparently it was up to me to state the obvious here. "Any ideas?"

"Excuse me," Octo-Cat said, still beaming proudly from behind his unsettling gift. I hadn't even realized he was paying attention. "I think I might have an idea," he said and then let out a contented chuckle.

He was back, baby!

CHAPTER NINETEEN

One week later...

My mom held a microphone to Nan's face, beaming at her with daughterly pride. "And to think, it only took you two weeks to plan this gorgeous affair."

My grandmother wore her hair in a French twist and sported a bold red lip. She'd even commissioned a special gown to wear to the gala. Silver beaded pawprints lined the neck and sleeves of her pink satin dress, creating a stunning effect.

Despite the quick event planning turn-around, it seemed all of Glendale had shown up to support Nan's fundraiser for the

Community Animal Shelter. Half the people from our neighboring towns, too. My mother and her cameraman had also shown up to film a human-interest piece for the local news.

Yeah, it was a pretty big deal.

While Mom interviewed Nan, I did another round through the house. Yes, we'd decided to use our own home as the location for the event tonight. Mr. Gables from the downtown council also helped to secure a series of large, impressive-looking tents, which we'd set up outside to expand the venue's workable space.

The charity gala included a catered dinner, silent auction, and the chance for attendees to write generous checks to support our shelter. We'd arranged to have all the VIP players inside the house so that it would be easier to keep an eye on them. If all went according to plan, we'd be able to oust a weasel before the night was through.

I'd chosen to wear a little black dress, so I could sneak around if it became necessary. A hands-free communications device had also been tucked into my ear so that Octo-Cat and I could keep each other updated throughout the evening. As long as I made it look like I was discussing something related to the gala, then I could speak freely and without question.

We'd blocked off the upstairs to discourage guests from exploring the upper floors and also to help hide Octo-Cat where he sat perched near the spindles that lined the hallway. His job was to watch the guests below and report what he saw via our FaceTime voice call.

He'd actually been the one to come up with the idea for tonight's ambush. Nan and I had just seen to the details. Paisley, too, by keeping everyone's spirits up with her constant optimism and kindness.

She believed the bad guy would be caught and that we would all win Detective once and for all.

And I chose to believe that, too.

"The eagle has landed," Octo-Cat rasped in my ear. He'd been joining Nan for her spy movie marathons lately and had picked up the lingo quickly. Since no one could understand him but me, I preferred he speak plainly—but

I guessed whatever made this fun for him was okay by me.

I turned toward the foyer just in time to see our target, the shelter's Community Outreach Coordinator, Mr. Leavitt, enter my home. He wore a very becoming black tux and an enormous grin that stretched from cheek to cheek.

"Hello, stranger," I said after I made my way over to him, hating the taste of those flirtatious words in my mouth. My heart belonged to Charles and Charles alone, but still I needed to get our prime suspect to play straight into my hands and was willing to do whatever it took.

Well, within reason, that is.

"You and your grandmother have really outdone yourselves," he exclaimed as I led him toward the cash bar we'd set up in the dining room. "This place looks fabulous!"

"It doesn't just look fabulous. It *is* fabulous," I responded right on cue. Nan and I had practiced my role in this charade many times, and while I didn't have an exact script, I knew all the points I was expected to hit as quickly and naturally as possible.

"We've already raised over twenty thousand dollars just from the table reservations alone. By the time the silent auctions and donations come in, we could be over one hundred thousand. Not bad for one night's work, huh?"

There, I'd said all the most important things. Nan would be so proud if she were here to witness my debut performance.

Mr. Leavitt's eyes widened with poorly concealed avarice. If he'd been carrying a drink, I imagine he may have choked on it. Instead, he merely stuttered his next words. "O-o-one hundred thousand dollars? You don't say."

"Oh, but I do." I placed a delicate hand on his shoulder and laughed. "It turns out people are very generous when it comes to saving the animals."

"Yes, I've always thought so."

The bartender handed him a glass of white wine and refilled my seltzer and lime. I wasn't much of a drinker under normal circumstances, but tonight I needed all my wits about me. I also needed to redirect Mr.

Leavitt to the foyer so that Octo-Cat could keep an eye on things as they went down.

"Excuse me for just a moment," I said, drawing my phone out of my strapless clutch and pushing send on the message that I had already composed earlier that evening.

Smiling up at Mr. Leavitt, I said, "There. Now that that's done, let's enjoy the party. I have so many people I'd like to introduce you to. Did you know Nan was a famous Broadway actress back in her glory days? She has many wealthy friends from her time in the city, and several of them came out to support her—to support the shelter—tonight."

"Fantastic," Mr. Leavitt said and took another sip from his glass.

A loud tapping followed by a burst of microphone interference filled the room, causing everyone to fall silent.

"Excuse me, excuse me, ladies and gentle-men," Nan cried into the mic. "I just wanted to say a huge thanks to a donor who asked to remain anonymous. She just gave us a fifty-thou-sand-dollar donation, single-handedly putting us over our fundraising goal for the evening.

Thanks to her big heart, the shelter can stay open for another two full years and we can help all of Glendale's stray pets find their forever homes."

Everyone clapped politely. Some even gasped in awe.

What an amazingly generous gift... had it been real.

"Oh, this night has already exceeded our wildest expectations," I gushed to Mr. Leavitt, continuing the carefully planned facade. "Nan and I had hoped our little gala would be a success, but we had no idea it would raise *so much* money."

Nan snaked through the crowd and joined the two of us in the foyer. "Mr. Leavitt," she enthused. "I wanted to hand you this check personally. A fifty-thousand-dollar donation. Can you believe it?" She pressed the check into his hand, which was my signal.

"A problem with the vegetarian dinner option?" I shrieked into my headpiece. "No, no, no. We can't have that, especially not at a fundraiser for animals. I'll be right there."

I pressed my Bluetooth device to imitate ending a call and then turned toward Nan with a panicked expression. "C'mon, I think this one might require both of us. It was nice seeing you again, Mr. Leavitt. Enjoy the rest of your evening."

"It's all you, bud," I mumbled into the headpiece as Nan and I rushed outside. "Operation Red Dot is in full swing."

CHAPTER TWENTY

As much as Octo-Cat had hated being tricked by the red dot when I had to capture him for our vet visit, that little moment of treachery served as the entire basis for our plan to catch Mr. Leavitt red-dot-handed.

"It's not about the red dot," Octo-Cat had waxed philosophically. "It's about what the red dot *represents.*"

He'd gone on to explain that, for cats, the red dot itself is irresistible and basically impossible to ignore. My cat then urged us to find Mr. Leavitt's red dot, and by that time Nan had already said it best: *Money is its own motive, whether you have it or not.*

From there, we flew full force into planning the charity gala and, with it, our master plan. So, the fifty-thousand-dollar donation was a total fraud. We had fake checks printed with a fake name and fake address and even a made-up account number, counting on our bad guy to do the bad thing and steal it.

Officer Bouchard had gone undercover in plain clothes to stake out the bank in Dewdrop Springs. At the end of the day, Mr. Leavitt had a decision to make. He could either continue to slowly embezzle funds from the failing animal shelter, or he could grab the big check and make a run for it. Our hope was that the fifty-thousand-dollar carrot—or red dot, using Octo-Cat's preferred analogy—was enough to encourage him to do the latter.

"He's leaving! He's leaving!" Octo-Cat cried inside my ear while I pretended to be busy examining a tray of broccoli florets.

"Text him," I told Nan, who had a text to Officer Bouchard ready to go on her phone. As much as I hated being left out of the action, my role in this ambush had officially ended.

"Good work, Octavius," I said before

removing my headpiece. After that, I pulled my phone out of my clutch and sent a quick text to Charles.

May I have this dance?

He found me a short while later, and together we swayed on my front lawn until the stars came out...

Actually, that would have been incredibly romantic, but we did have to face one minor distraction first.

"He's got him." I heard Nan's words only moments before I felt her arms wrap around me from behind. She joined Charles and me in our dance as she whispered in my ear. "That fool went to the same exact bank as before. Turns out it had been him the whole time, except for the last two checks, of course. I'll tell you more when I know more." She gave me a kiss on the cheek and then wandered off.

"Your nan just pinched my butt," Charles told me with a laugh.

"Nan's gotta Nan," I responded, rolling my eyes. She and I could have a talk about boundaries later. Right now I wanted to enjoy my evening held tightly in Charles's strong arms.

"How'd you know it wasn't Trish?" he asked me.

"It was too perfect," I murmured, ready to put this whole thing behind me and enjoy the rest of the gala as best I could.

"Kind of like you," he said, giving me a quick kiss on the cheek.

"Yeah, sure," I joked, but snuggled closer to him all the same. If he wanted to believe I was perfect, then I refused to stop him.

It was Harmony of all people who finally gave the info that would solve the case. Remember that mean masseuse? Yeah, her.

Turns out Trish had visited Serenity day spa because Stone—whose real name was Declan—also worked at the Dewdrop Springs branch of the First Bank of Blueberry Bay. He'd helped Mr. Leavitt cash his stolen checks and then frame Trish for it.

And Harmony—whose real name was truly and legitimately Harmony—heard enough to testify against him. From there, he cracked wide open and confessed everything.

Paisley hadn't seen Trish before because Trish didn't technically work for the shelter. The sweet but forgetful front desk attendant Pearl was her grandmother, and for weeks Mr. Leavitt had been threatening to let her go due to her age and the suspicion she had early onset dementia. He'd used that threat along with a few carefully constructed lies to con Trish into carrying out his dirty work.

And when he sensed me and Nan hot on his tail, he set Trish up to take the fall for all of it. He'd sent her to cash the checks with Stone. He'd also sent her to buy the stolen supplies, instructing his lackey to purposefully end up in the wrong lot and force her to walk all about town with the hopes someone would discover her suspicious behavior.

And, yeah, I'd played right into his hand.

If it weren't for my pets and that disgusting dead mouse, I may have never realized that we'd accused the wrong person.

Luckily, my pets *were* gross, and Mr. Leavitt —whose first name is Alex, by the way— would be going away for a long, long time.

Now someone who really believes in the animal shelter's mission will be taking over as the Community Outreach Coordinator.

Pearl.

A doctor quickly dismissed the dementia diagnosis and ruled her completely in good health and of sound mind. So now, she runs things, and her devoted granddaughter Trish has taken over as the first face you see when entering the facility.

Nan and I, for our part, plan to continue organizing fundraisers to help the shelter get back on its feet.

So I guess you can say we all lived happily ever after.

Well, until the next case anyway…

WHAT'S NEXT?

Lately my life has seemed pretty perfect—great house, great gig as my own boss, great new boyfriend, and the world's most awesome talking cat. Turns out I shouldn't have let my guard down...

Even though my private investigation firm is brand new, I've already got some not-so-friendly competition, and it's coming from the sticky-fingered raccoon who lives under my front porch. I have no doubt he's robbing his clients, since he's stealing from mine, too.

Things go from irritating to downright dangerous when he foists a little trinket from my attic, one that suggests dark secrets and spells big trouble for my beloved Nan.

I need to learn more, but that's not going to be easy since the person of interest lives under the same roof. Can I trust this raccoon racketeer with something so dear? Unfortunately, I haven't got any other options.

Pre-order to save! RACCOON RACKETEER is just $2.99 until it releases on October 24.

Get your copy here!
mollymysteries.com/RaccoonR

SNEAK PEEK: RACCOON RACKETEER

Hey, my name's Angie Russo, and I own one-half of a private investigation firm here in beautiful Blueberry Bay, Maine.

The other half belongs to my cat, Octavius—or Octo-Cat for short. It may not seem like his nickname keeps things short, but trust me on that one. Every time he tells anyone his full name, he always adds at least one new title to the end. The most recent version is Octavius Maxwell Ricardo Edmund Frederick Fulton Russo, Esq. P.I.

Like I said, it's a mouthful.

And he's kind of a handful, too.

While my spoiled tabby is undoubtedly my

best friend, he does have a way of making my life harder. For instance, he's been catnapped, ordered to court for arbitration, and even repeatedly threatened to kill our new dog.

Did I mention that all happened in the span of just one month?

But that's Octo-Cat for you.

Love him or hate him, there's no denying he's a true individual.

And even though he's just about as stubborn as they come, he does occasionally change his mind about things.

That new dog we adopted? She's a sweet rescue Chihuahua named Paisley. She liked him from the start, but it took Octo-Cat much longer to warm up to her. Now I am proud to report that the two have become close friends. One of my cat's favorite hobbies has become stalking and pouncing on his dog and then wrestling her to the ground.

Yes, *his* dog. That's how much the tables have turned in these past few weeks.

Together, the three of us live with my grandmother, Nan. Although she's the main one who raised me, she lives in my house.

And I live in my cat's house.

Yup, Octo-Cat is a trust fund kitty, and his stipend is more than generous enough to pay the mortgage on our exquisite New England manor house.

It's a bit ridiculous, I'll be the first to admit that. But, hey, when life gives you lemonade, it's best if you drink up and enjoy!

Speaking of, I've been dating my dream guy for about seven weeks now. His name is Charles Longfellow, III, and he's my dream guy for good reason. Not only is he the sole partner at the law firm where I used to work, but he's also incredibly smart, kind, attentive —and, okay, I may as well just admit it—sexy.

Not that we've…

Anyway!

I can talk to my cat. I probably should have mentioned that earlier, seeing as it's the most unusual thing about me.

I can talk to my dog, too, and most animals now.

Long story short, I got electrocuted at a will reading, and when I regained conscious-ness, I heard Octo-Cat making fun of me.

Once he realized I could understand him, he recruited me to solve his late owner's murder, and the rest is history.

From there, we realized two things. One, we make a really good crime-solving team, and two, we were stuck with each other for better or worse. Usually, things are better, but he still has his hissy fits on occasion—and so do I, for that matter.

And I guess that brings me to today.

Today marks the two-month mark since we first opened our P.I. outfit for business, and in that time, we've had exactly zero clients. Even my normally optimistic nan can't spin this one in a positive light.

No one wants to hire us, and I'm not sure why.

I'm well-liked in town, and it's not like people know I can actually talk to animals. They think including my cat as a partner is just a gimmick, and I prefer it that way, honestly.

But I'm starting to worry that we'll never bring any business in.

At what point do we give up on our entrepreneurial enterprise?

Octo-Cat is pretty happy sleeping in the sun most of the day, but I prefer to have more in my life. I even quit my former job as a paralegal to make sure I had enough time for all the investigative work I felt certain would fall into my lap the moment we opened for business.

Yeah, I was more than a little wrong about that one.

I need to figure out something, and fast, if I want to keep my operation afloat, but how can I trust my instincts when they were so wrong before?

Here's hoping Octo-Cat has a bright idea he'd be willing to share...

It was Wednesday morning, and I'd spent the better part of the last two days handing out flyers to any person, business, or animal who would take one. Out of desperation, I'd even visited parking lots and shoved the brightly colored papers touting my credentials under the windshield wipers of each car in the lot.

Still, not one person had called to share a case with me.

Not one.

Nan had left the house early to serve a volunteer shift picking up litter around town. We'd both agreed the animal shelter, while in need, wasn't the best place for her to share her generous heart—because we both knew she'd end up adopting almost every dog and cat in that place.

Our house was already full enough, thank you very much.

I sat in the front room of the house, sipping a can of Diet Coke. The coffee maker still scared me silly, given that the last time I'd used one I'd been electrocuted, and tea just wasn't the same without Nan to keep me company.

Paisley and Octo-Cat scampered around the house in their perpetual game of tag, and I wracked my brain for any kind of idea that would help get us some clients.

The electronic pet door buzzed, and both animals ran outside.

I smiled and watched them zigzag through

the yard. Mid-autumn had hit Maine, and now most of the fire-colored leaves had fallen from the trees. While I tried my best to keep up with the raking, it wasn't easy given the fact that an enormous forest flanked my property on two sides.

Leaves blew into our yard all the time.

Like right now.

I sighed as a gust so strong I could practically see it swept through the trees and deposited at least five landscaping bags full of leaves on the front lawn. Leaves of every color carpeted the greenish yellow grass—red, orange, yellow… turquoise?

"Mommy! Mommy!" Paisley cried from outside, and I went running. The sweet and innocent Chihuahua got upset fairly easily, but her small size also made her incredibly vulnerable. I never took any chances when it came to her safety, and neither did Nan or Octo-Cat.

One of us was always with her whenever she ventured outside.

And even though I knew Octo-Cat was out there now, I still needed to make sure nothing had happened to frighten her.

Both Paisley and Octo-Cat were waiting for me on the porch when I stepped outside. Paisley even had a turquoise piece of paper clamped within her jaws.

"What's this?" I asked, taking it from her.

"It's one of your papers, Mommy!" the little dog cried proudly.

I glanced at the bright paper in my hands and then back out to the yard where dozens, maybe even hundreds, more had mixed with the autumnal leaves.

She was right. This was my paper. In fact, it was the flyer for our P.I. firm that I had so painstakingly distributed the last couple of days. I'd handed out every single one that Nan had printed for us—I'd made sure of it.

So why had they all followed me home?

And how?

A squeaky laugh underneath the porch gave me a pretty good idea.

"Pringle!" I yelled, stomping my feet as hard as I could to try to force the raccoon out of there.

I knew he was mad at me ever since I'd banned him from entering the house, but to sabotage my business? Really?

Pre-order to save! RACCOON RACKETEER is just $2.99 until it releases on October 24.

Get your copy here!
mollymysteries.com/RaccoonR

WHAT'S AFTER THAT?

Ever feel like your entire world has been turned on its head? That's how I've felt ever since the gang and I found out that Nan has been keeping major family secrets stashed neatly away in the attic.

What's worse, she won't stop talking about them now that they're out in the open. I still have so many questions, though, like is she still the same woman I always assumed she was? And can I ever fully trust her again?

When Nan refuses to give me a straight answer, I invite my parents to join me for a cross-country train trip so that we can all discover the truth, once and for all.

Octo-Cat hitches a ride with us, too, and

it's a good thing he does, because it isn't long before a dead body joins us in the dining car. Now we have two mysteries to solve, and fast —our lives and legacy depend on it.

Pre-order to save! HIMALAYAN HAZARD is just $2.99 until it releases on November 14.

Get your copy here!
mollymysteries.com/HimalayanH

MORE FROM BLUEBERRY BAY

Welcome to Blueberry Bay, a scenic region of Maine peppered with quaint small towns and home to a shocking number of mysteries. If you loved this book, then make sure to check out its sister series from other talented Cozy Mystery authors...

Pet Whisperer P.I.
By Molly Fitz

Glendale is home to Blueberry Bay's first ever talking cat detective. Along with his ragtag gang of human and animal helpers, Octo-Cat is determined to save the day… so long as it doesn't interfere with his schedule. Start with book one, *Kitty Confidential*, which is now available to buy or borrow! Visit Visit www.QuirkyCozy.com/PetWhisperer for more.

Little Dog Diner
By Emmie Lyn

Misty Harbor boasts the best lobster rolls in all of Blueberry Bay. There's another thing that's always on the menu, too. Murder! Dani and her little terrier, Pip, have a knack for being in the wrong place at the wrong time… which often lands them smack in the middle of a fresh, new murder mystery and in the crosshairs of one cunning criminal after the next. Start with book one, *Mixing Up Murder*, which is now available to buy or borrow! Visit www.QuirkyCozy.com/LittleDog for more.

Shelf Indulgence
By S.E. Babin

Dewdrop Springs is home to Tattered Pages, a popular bookshop with an internet cafe, a grumpy Persian cat named Poppy, and some of the most suspicious characters you'll ever meet. And poor Dakota Adair has just inherited it all. She'll need to make peace with her new cat and use all her book smarts to catch a killer or she might be the next to wind up dead in the stacks. Book one, *Hardback Homicide*, will be coming soon. Keep an eye on www.QuirkyCozy.com for more.

Haunted Housekeeping
By R.A. Muth

Cooper's Cove is home to Blueberry Bay's premier estate cleaning service. Tori and Hazel, the ill-fated proprietors of Bubbles and Troubles, are prepared to uncover a few skeletons. But when a real one turns up, they'll have to solve the mystery quickly if they're going to save their reputations—and their lives. Book one, *The Squeaky Clean Skeleton*, will be coming soon. Keep an eye on www.QuirkyCozy.com for more.

The Kindergarten Coven
By F.M. Storm

Quiet, secluded, and most importantly, far away from his annoying magical family, Guy couldn't wait to start a new life on Caraway Island. Unfortunately, he hadn't counted on his four-year-old daughter coming into her own witchy powers early… or on her accidentally murdering one of the PTO moms. Oops! Book one, *Stay-at-Home Sorcery*, will be coming soon. Keep an eye on www.QuirkyCozy.com for more.

ABOUT MOLLY FITZ

While USA Today bestselling author Molly Fitz can't technically talk to animals, she and her doggie best friend, Sky Princess, have deep and very animated conversations as they navigate their days. Add to that, five more dogs, a snarky feline, comedian husband, and diva daughter, and you can pretty much imagine how life looks at the Casa de Fitz.

Molly lives in a house on a high hill in the Michigan woods and occasionally ventures out for good food, great coffee, or to meet new animal friends.

Writing her quirky, cozy animal mysteries is pretty much a dream come true, but she also goes by the name Melissa Storm (also a USA Today bestselling author, yay!) and writes a very different kind of story.

Learn more, grab the free app, or sign up for her newsletter at www.MollyMysteries.com!

MORE FROM MOLLY

If you're ready to dive right in to more Pet Whisperer P.I., then you can even order the other books right now by clicking below:

Kitty Confidential

Terrier Transgressions

Hairless Harassment

Dog-Eared Delinquent

The Cat Caper

Chihuahua Conspiracy

Raccoon Racketeer

Himalayan Hazard

Hoppy Holiday Homicide

Retriever Ransom

Lawless Litter

Legal Seagull

Pet Whisperer P.I. Books 1-3

Six Merry Little Murders

CONNECT WITH MOLLY

Sign up for Molly's newsletter for book updates and cat pics: **mollymysteries.com/subscribe**

Download Molly's app for cool bonus content: **mollymysteries.com/app**

Join Molly's reader group on Facebook to make new friends: **mollymysteries.com/group**

Made in the USA
Monee, IL
14 April 2021

65739180R00121